"I saw him again last night," Wes told her.

Her head shot toward him. "What?" Her eyes were full of worry and also maybe a little anger.

"I went out on the front porch with my rifle and he turned and left," he said.

Indie sighed and ran her fingers through her long hair.

"I think you should come and stay at my ranch until your investigation is over," he suggested grimly. "I have a den that also functions as a second office. The killer doesn't know me or where I live. You'll be safe there."

Indie sat at her table, putting down her cup and staring into the dark liquid. "I'll admit, having a stalker who might be the killer I'm after is unsettling, but as I've mentioned before, I'm trained for this, Wes. You really don't have to worry about me."

"Then I can keep staying here. Call it being overprotective, but I don't want any other man doing that for you."

Dear Reader,

I've been writing my Cold Case Detectives series for some time now. It seems readers enjoy them, which makes me so happy. The stories have spanned a few states and a few have been set in Texas. Texas intrigues me, and *Cold Case Cowboy* epitomizes the West. Indiana Deboe (I love her last name, don't ask me why) is stationed in the Irving/Dallas area and I continued to focus on sexy cowboys, but it is time to move on to other settings for future books. Her story is a great transition for this.

The core character theme for *Cold Case Cowboy* is the hero and heroine have a real connection with past family tragedies. It is what brings them together, along with the perilous pursuit of a serial killer. May you fall into their journey, both in love and danger.

For my next book, look forward to another female Dark Alley Investigations PI who returns to her roots in Calgary, Alberta, Canada, with the Canadian Rockies as a backdrop.

My best, always.

Jennifer Morey

COLD CASE
COWBOY

Jennifer Morey

HARLEQUIN®
ROMANTIC SUSPENSE™

Recycling programs
for this product may
not exist in your area.

ISBN-13: 978-1-335-75975-7

Cold Case Cowboy

Copyright © 2022 by Jennifer Morey

Harlequin Enterprises ULC
22 Adelaide St. West, 41st Floor
Toronto, Ontario M5H 4E3, Canada
www.Harlequin.com

Printed in U.S.A.

Two-time RITA® Award nominee and Golden Quill award winner **Jennifer Morey** writes single-title contemporary romance and page-turning romantic suspense. She has a geology degree and has managed export programs in compliance with the International Traffic in Arms Regulations (ITAR) for the aerospace industry. She lives at the foot of the Rocky Mountains in Denver, Colorado, and loves to hear from readers through her website, jennifermorey.com, or Facebook.

Books by Jennifer Morey

Harlequin Romantic Suspense

Cold Case Detectives

A Wanted Man
Justice Hunter
Cold Case Recruit
Taming Deputy Harlow
Runaway Heiress
Hometown Detective
Cold Case Manhunt
Her P.I. Protector
Cold Case Cowboy

Colton 911: Chicago

Colton 911: Temptation Undercover

The Coltons of Mustang Valley

Colton Family Bodyguard

Visit the Author Profile page at Harlequin.com for more titles.

For Mom

Chapter 1

Indie Deboe stood by herself at Julien Lacroix and Skylar Chelsey's engagement party. The Chelseys' ranch was near Waldon, a small town north of Irving, Texas. Julien had invited a few other private detectives from Dark Alley Investigations, but so far no one else from the agency had shown up. After having been here a while already, she'd begun to feel out of place when she spotted a man looking at her. Wes McCann, she remembered, having been briefly introduced to him earlier. Also standing alone, he was tall and dark-haired, and had an intimidating presence. Big and fit. There were a lot of cowboys at this party, as evidenced by all the hats, but this one stood out for some reason. He was good-looking in a rugged way.

She decided to go over and say hello. Not that she

was actively looking for a boyfriend—quite the opposite, in fact. But she might as well mingle while she was here. Besides, they were apparently both solo.

The handsome cowboy watched her approach, and his gaze ran down the length of her before returning to her face. He didn't appear to mind that she saw him do that. *Bold man*.

A few tingles ran through her, not missing his obviously sexual observation. Her excited reaction caught her a little off guard.

"You look like you need company as much as I do," she said. "Indie Deboe."

He reached out to shake her hand. "Wes McCann. We met." He had amazing light blue eyes.

She smiled. "I remember," she said.

"You have a nice name."

She liked how genuine his words sounded when he said that. His blue button up shirt tightened around his muscular shoulders and biceps as he leaned on the table. Drawn to him too much and too fast, she asked, "Are any of these people your friends or do you just prefer to be alone?"

That caused one side of his mouth to crook up—ever so slightly. Then he glanced around. "Neighbors. And yes."

He preferred to be alone? Was he a lone wolf? Or...

"Going through a rough patch?" she asked.

"Exactly."

His ready admission suggested he was more of a straight shooter than someone who would keep secrets or be deceptive. She decided to see how far he'd go in his honesty.

"What happened? Was it a woman?"

"My wife left me. I saw it coming but that doesn't make it any easier," he said, just a hint of regret tinging his tone.

"I'm sorry. I do know relationships can be unpredictable." For her, *unpredictable* didn't really adequately describe her experiences. She'd struggled in the past with interpreting men's real intentions regarding her, or ascertaining whether they were worth the time. Indie blamed it on the way her childhood had ended abruptly. She had lost her parents and sister at a young age and hadn't had any real guidance in making her way through adulthood, particularly the emotional side, in finding and connecting with a man.

A sigh escaped her. She probably should not have approached Wes. Indie knew she did that a lot, striking up a conversation and then, when things slid beyond her control, suddenly finding herself stuck in a violent relationship.

"You've had your share?" he asked.

"Don't we all?" She kept it light, but deep down inside, the old feeling of impending failure fought to resurface.

Wes grinned, but only slightly, and she suspected he didn't feel the joy in it. "Yes, I suppose so. My mistake was rushing into my second marriage too fast. My first wife died."

Again, he sounded matter-of-fact, as though he could easily talk about this without feeling pain. Most likely he had a pretty stout wall erected around his heart right now. Indie could definitely relate to that after experiencing her own challenges in the relationship department. She struggled against letting that endear him to her, but it didn't seem to be working.

"Oh," she said. "I'm so sorry…again."

At this point, she should say a polite farewell and never look back. She wasn't the type of woman who felt compelled to fix broken men. Unfortunately, broken men were the only ones she found herself drawn to. She couldn't afford another one. But Wes's forthrightness captured her fascination. That and those intriguing blue eyes. More than their brilliance, she saw the will to stave off pain. And something else. Strength. How did she know? Just call it intuition.

"How old are you?" she asked. "You have me curious, that's all."

His lips quirked up again. "You had me curious from the moment you walked into the room."

"One look gave you all that?"

"Call it intuition," he murmured.

The fact that he said that made her breathe a laugh. What were the odds? Did he think he read people as well as he seemed to?

"Well, we were the only two people standing alone in a room full of people. Doesn't that say enough right there?"

When he chuckled, his entire face changed. Not the ruggedness, but his eyes lit up and a row of healthy white teeth flashed.

Wow.

"You're a funny girl. I haven't married one of those yet," he said lightly.

Married? Why had he said that? He must be joking.

"I'm thirty-six. And you are…?" he asked.

"Thirty-one. Married once." What she would never say was what a whopper that experience had been. One of those failures that hung on for a lifetime. Enough for her.

"Is there a reason it didn't work out?" he prompted. "It can't be because of your long blond hair and those gorgeous aqua blue eyes." His gaze moved down her body again. "Or the rest of it."

Oh, gosh. He was so brazen! A laugh bubbled up.

"The man must be a complete fool," he added.

Indie almost faltered at that. She had not been blameless in the downfall of her marriage, but, she admitted to herself, neither had she loved her ex-husband as much as she should have. "Then it must be my tendency to work from the moment I wake up to the time I close my eyes at night." That should placate Wes enough, at least for now. She was grateful for the fun banter at a party where she was otherwise alone. Talking about her divorce usually ended with her in a puddle of tears.

"How did you come to be invited to this shindig?" he asked.

"I work for Dark Alley Investigations. I'm a private detective."

He nodded. "Ah. Like Julien."

She laughed again. "Yes. He and I work together."

"Maybe I should turn tail and run right now." His eyes were mesmerizing when they twinkled like that.

"I was thinking the same about you." She was beginning to hope he wouldn't run, actually. In fact, she was starting to think she'd like to see more of him.

One of the waiters brought him another shot of what appeared to be whiskey.

Indie observed him a moment and then put her glass of wine down. "You know, numbing your sorrows doesn't usually work."

"It will for now." Another faint, crooked grin lifted his mouth. Cynical. Unapologetic. He clearly walked his own path, and had no care about what others thought of him.

This might be too soon to ask, but he had already been so blunt she didn't see a reason not to. "So why did your marriage fail?" She was ready to return his truth with another equally forthright question.

"To be honest, I have no idea. One day I thought she loved me and everything was fine and the next she went to her parents' house, and now we are getting a divorce. Already filed."

He was still married? Technically, although he had already filed and it would soon be finalized. But still… Wes had said he married too soon after his first wife's death. Surely that had something to do with it, if not everything?

Again, this was where most women would say a polite farewell and be on their way. He was obviously still too emotionally raw—plus, he was still legally someone else's husband—to be a prospect for her. She wasn't looking for one anyway. Right? She sighed again. Why did she have to keep reminding herself of that? He wasn't ready and neither was she.

"She didn't tell you why she left?" Indie continued.

"She left without telling me anything. She didn't want me to find her. I would have, but her parents lied about her staying there."

He would have found her? "And done what?"

"Profess my love. I'm a hopeless romantic." He sounded cynical again.

She blew out a laugh. "You are not a hopeless romantic. You can't be." She gave him a once-over. "You look like a tough, ranch-man womanizer." Cowboy hat, tanned skin like he spent much of his time in the sun, subtle wrinkles around his eyes…

"Looks can be deceiving," he reminded her.

"Are you still in love with your soon-to-be ex-wife?" she asked.

"No."

While she pondered over the calm and deliberate way he said that, someone appeared next to her. It was Julien.

"Is this guy bothering you?" he teased.

"No. We were just having a deep conversation."

Although he didn't grin or laugh, Wes's eyes glimmered with delight. It was hardly a deep conversation.

Indie gestured to Wes and then said to Julien, "I assume you know each other?"

"Yes, we do. How are you?" Julien asked Wes.

"Doing well."

"Thanks for stopping by," Julien said.

"I figured it was time to get more social."

"If I'm not interrupting, why don't you tell me about your latest case?" Julien said, turning to her. "I heard it could be a difficult one to solve."

"Who told you I have one?"

"When do you *not* have one?" He chuckled. "You never stop working."

Indie caught Wes's look. Julien had just confirmed she had told the truth.

"It was Kadin who told me about the case," Julien said.

Kadin Tandy had started Dark Alley Investigations after the murder of his daughter. Since then, it had grown into a large, nationwide, and in some cases international, private investigations agency. After a career in the local police department, Indie had needed a change and joined DAI. Working for the agency satisfied her need to seek justice, whether or not a case was deemed cold.

"A body was found in a remote area of a Dallas park. She was naked and had on a blindfold. There's evidence of rape and she was stabbed nine times." It was okay to reveal details of the case that had already been reported in the news in front of a stranger.

"No leads?" Julien asked.

"None. Police already interviewed everyone close to her. I plan on revisiting them."

"Who was she?" Wes interjected. "What do the police know?"

"Her name is Mya Berry. She was twenty-four and has a four-year-old daughter," she rattled off. "Not married, but she was divorced. The ex has an alibi. Her car was found at home, locked. The house was dark and also locked. Her purse and car keys are missing. She had gone out that night. Her friends said she left the bar at eleven. None of the neighbors saw her come home or anything else. Her daughter was at her parents' house for the night."

She cleared her throat before continuing. "It looks like she either went willingly or was abducted by someone right outside her house, before she even entered, so somewhere between her car and the front door. Police said her ex-boyfriend is a person of interest, since he says he was at home during the time Mya disappeared. He's not a suspect because he broke things off with her and kept saying how nice she was. He had no reason to kill her. People close to him and Mya corroborated that."

"Why did he break it off?" Julien asked curiously.

"That's what I to want to look into," she answered. "Police report said he thought she was too quiet for him. Not much stimulating conversation. And also that she had a child."

"Where is the girl now?" Wes murmured.

Indie thought she detected a note of concern in his voice. Maybe this tough cowboy had a soft side after all? "She's still with Mya's parents."

Wes wore a grim frown, as though he felt sorry for the child. Did he ever want kids of his own? The notion tickled her curiosity, even as she dismissed it.

"Yeah, when there are kids involved that part of the job gets hard to deal with," Julien admitted.

"But makes me work that much more tenaciously to find the bad guy," Indie said. She hadn't yet met the little girl but it had to be difficult for everyone.

"Who contacted DAI for help?" Julien asked.

"Mya's parents. After police informed her the case went cold, which was months later."

Julien nodded. "Well, I'm sure you'll find a thread to pull. If you need any help, let me know."

"Will do." Indie went quiet, reminded of something that had changed in her life recently.

"You look like you already have one," Julien said. "What's the matter?"

She shook her head. "Nothing. I've been getting these weird calls. Always on my work phone and always traced to a burner phone."

"What kind of calls?" Wes asked, looking concerned.

"Nothing specific. The person on the other end never says anything. Just stays on the line while I say hello. Then hangs up. I traced the mobile equipment identifier—the MEID—to a cell tower near the park where Mya's body was found. Then tried tracing the MEID to a store where the phone might have been purchased, but no luck there. The person—maybe it's the same person who killed Mya—probably buys his phones on a street corner." The whole point of having a burner phone was anonymity.

"Sounds like the criminal might be nervous DAI was hired," Julien said.

Indie didn't say anything. The idea that a murderer possibly knew who she was, how to contact her, and didn't want her fishing for evidence made her uneasy. Sure, due to her police training, she was good with her gun and knew how defend herself, but she didn't know anything yet about this killer, least of all what he looked like or where to find him. She wouldn't know him if he stood right in front of her.

Julien's fiancée, Skylar, approached. She leaned toward Julien and he kissed her tenderly. Indie saw how Skylar looked at him, and could feel her love. Indie had never felt an emotion that potent before. She'd thought her ex-husband, Cole, had been the one, but she couldn't have been more wrong. She didn't know it wasn't true love until it was too late.

Wes's masculine good looks reminded her that she would not allow herself to be wrong again.

Wes McCann saw how apprehensive Indie looked, talking about being stalked, and felt a sudden urge to keep her safe. It took him off guard. A woman like Indie Deboe did not need protecting. He didn't know anything about her, but to be a detective at an agency like DAI, she had to be seasoned.

He supposed part of the reason for his instinct was how her beauty struck him the moment he saw her. Blonde hair, blue-eyed and slender, fit body, with just the right sized breasts. And there was something else, the way she looked at him. He saw strength and interest in her gaze. But, oh, getting embroiled in another romantic entanglement was the last thing he should be doing right now. In fact, it would be totally bad

for him. Nothing like making the same mistake—
getting attracted to the wrong woman—yet again…

It was time for him to go. He'd had enough social
interaction to last him the rest of the week, and he
decided to make a hasty exit. As he made his way to
the door, he saw Indie also headed out.

She glanced back and then did a double take. "Nice
meeting you, Wes," she said with a beautiful smile.

"Nice meeting you," he said. *Too nice.*

He averted his gaze from her delectable rear and
caught sight of a running car among the throng of
others parked in the spacious circular driveway. A
man was sitting inside and looking right at Indie. He
wore a baseball hat and sunglasses, even though it
was dark and going on ten at night.

Wes pretended not to notice and wondered if Indie
did the same. Or had she been distracted by seeing
Wes again and aware of him behind her?

He got into his truck and waited for her to drive
away. *Just to make sure she leaves safely*, he told
himself.

But as she left, the man in the car followed. Was
this the killer?

Careful to keep his distance, Wes trailed behind
Indie and the stranger all the way into Irving, where
the pretty PI drove to what had to be her home. It was
a newer neighborhood with houses that he estimated
to be about twenty-five hundred to three thousand
square feet. She pulled into a driveway. The stranger
parked along the side of the street. Wes passed him,
turned the next corner and parked out of sight. He'd

wait to see what the stranger did. He knew Indie could take care of herself but the man in him intended to stop this person before he had a chance to reach her.

Wes watched as the man got out of his car, now wearing a mask. The guy checked his pistol as if to see whether it was ready to fire. Then the intruder started for Indie's house.

This might be an extreme idea. He chased animals away from livestock, not people away from other people. Heart pumping as he refused to turn back, Wes alighted from his truck, Wes grabbed the rifle on a rack in the back seat of his truck and sprinted toward Indie's house. He ran up Indie's driveway and kept to the shrubbery as he crept around to the back. Peering around the corner, he spotted the stranger checking the back sliding door. It was locked. He checked the windows.

The man's head whipped in his direction. Seeing the rifle, the interloper turned and bolted. Wes chased him to the front of the house and down the driveway, mindful of the pistol. The man glanced back a couple of times as he ran, but never fired. He reached his car and the tires squealed as he raced away. Wes stood in the middle of the street and watched with the rifle lowered until the car vanished.

Then he walked up the driveway to Indie's front door, which opened before he could ring the bell.

Indie looked around, her brow lowered.

"You were followed home. He was armed," he said.

"I saw that a man was tailing me," she replied

grimly. Wes wondered when she had noticed the guy. Likely soon after leaving the Chelseys'.

Stepping past her, he entered before she invited him. No way was he leaving her alone tonight. Sure, she was capable of protecting herself, but as a man he couldn't step aside and do nothing.

"Come on in," Indie said, sassing him but in a lighthearted way.

"Someone just followed you home," he repeated. Propping the rifle against the wall next to the door, he faced her. "I'm not leaving you alone."

She looked down and then back up dubiously. "I'm trained for this."

"I know you're experienced and capable, but I can't, in good conscience, abandon you as though nothing dangerous just happened."

Wordlessly, she walked from the wide entryway where a stairway led up to the second level. He followed her around the stairs through a living and dining room, through an expansive arch leading to the kitchen. She went about filling a teakettle with water and then put it on the stove.

At last she leaned against the counter and looked at him.

"I don't even know you," she said.

"I'd feel the same if I had never exchanged any words with someone who was being stalked by a deadly man. Do you think it was the killer you're trying to apprehend?"

"Yes," she said, biting her lower lip briefly.

She struck him as a woman who rarely showed

emotion, someone toughened by life and her profession. Sort of like him...

"It could also be a random stalker," he mused.

Even as the words left Wes's mouth, he knew it didn't matter who it was. If he hadn't been there to chase him away, what would have happened? She had watched from the window and had been prepared with her pistol. If Wes needed help, she would have been more than ready.

"I'm not working any other cases. There's no one else it could be." She averted her head as though a thought came to her.

"Anyone in your personal life?" he asked.

After a moment she shrugged. "I've had relationships that ended badly but I don't think any of them would have it out for me like that. And it's been almost a year since I've seen anyone."

From what little he knew, Wes doubted the stalker was someone from her past. So he was inclined to agree with Indie's assessment. It made more sense that it was the killer she was after and the threat she presented working for an agency like DAI. He realized she was experienced and knew what to do if danger came her way, but she could have been harmed or murdered tonight, were it not for Wes scaring the person away. And the idea of this woman—whom he'd just met—being killed shook him to his core.

"Maybe you should let the police take it from here," he said. "Or involve them."

"I can handle it. And I do involve them where necessary with our cases. We have to in order to protect any evidence we find." She looked at him as though doubt followed her words. Turning, she retrieved two cups from the cabinet.

"Sorry, I don't have any alcohol," she said.

"I've had enough." He liked a good whiskey or two every once in a while, but his drinking was not out of control.

She put teabags in the cups without asking if he wanted any. He wasn't a tea drinker but he'd have one with her.

"So you know the Chelseys?" she asked.

He sensed her need to move the subject on to something else. The low set of her brow and tense line of her mouth told him plenty. Wes doubted that much scared her but being followed apparently had. He imagined that not knowing for certain who the man had been and maybe speculating it could be Mya's killer made it worse.

"Yes. I'm a neighbor. I breed horses and rent out some land for neighboring ranchers to graze their livestock," he said.

The tension in her brow eased as though she had relaxed a little. "That brings in enough to run a whole ranch?"

"I have an inheritance from my grandparents and some from my own parents," he said.

"Have you always lived on a ranch?" she asked.

"No. I spent summers at my grandparents' ranch and joined the air force after high school."

"Oh. You were a pilot?" Her face lit up with interest.

"Yes. I flew F-22s mostly."

"Wow. Fighter jet pilot turned rancher."

He grinned. "I grew out of that stage of my life. What about you? How'd you turn to homicide investigations?"

"I went to college and graduated with a master's in criminal justice. I was a cop first, then a detective for the Dallas PD, before finding out about DAI," she said. "It pays more…and I like the challenge of cold cases."

The way she hesitated made him wonder if there was more than a challenge that drove her into solving these kinds of cases. "Are you from here?" he asked.

"No. I'm originally from Montana. I moved here when I went to college at Sam Houston State University in Huntsville. I moved to Dallas when I got my first job."

"Montana, huh? Quite a bit different than Texas."

"Yes. Sometimes I miss the mountains. I don't miss the cold, though." She smiled and handed him a steaming cup of tea.

"You must go back every once in a while. I assume your family still lives there?"

Her smile faded. Something about that didn't go over very well with her.

"I'm an only child," she said.

Didn't she visit her parents? Why did he want to know?

"I'm an only child, too," he told her gruffly. Enough about family. He didn't like talking about that any more than Indie apparently did. Putting his cup down, he went to the back door and looked out-side. Seeing no movement, he went to the front and peered out the living room window. Nothing there, either. Facing the room, he saw Indie had followed, sipping her tea and watching him. The room was co-zily decorated in grays and white. The couch looked long enough to fit him and fairly comfortable.

"I could sleep on your couch," he offered.

She swatted her hand down in a gesture of dis-missal. "Oh… I'll be all right."

"If not for you, then for me," he said. "I wouldn't feel I was doing my part otherwise." While his tone was half-teasing, he actually meant it. He wanted to make sure Indie was safe.

She met his eyes soberly for a moment. "Okay." She put down her cup on the coffee table. "I'll get some bedding."

While she went to get the items, Wes clicked on the television. He found an old Western and kept the volume low. The slight noise always helped him sleep. Although he doubted he'd get much sleep tonight. Be-tween wariness of a murderer lurking and thoughts of Indie, he'd have plenty to keep him alert. And he had a ranch to run.

Indie reappeared and began making a bed for him.

"Is Indie your real name?" he asked curiously.

"Indiana, but I'd rather not go by the name of a state."

He chuckled. He couldn't blame her. "I don't go by Weston, either."

She glanced back at him and smiled. Finished with the bed, she straightened. "Well, it's getting late…"

"Yes," he said, meeting her eyes.

He found he could not look away. Something sparked with the eye contact and an impulse to kiss her came over him.

She might have experienced the same, as she lowered her eyes briefly at his gaze. "Well, good night."

"Good night."

After she disappeared up the stairs, Wes felt a surge of disappointment. Still, he pulled the sheet and blanket back and reclined on the couch, arm behind his head on the pillow.

Yup, it was going to be a long, long night.

Chapter 2

Indie lay in bed unable to sleep, knowing a man was in her living room. One she had just met earlier tonight. Worse, although she had gotten good vibes from him, she refused to trust herself anymore when it came to picking men. For almost an hour now, she had been mulling over that. Why had she agreed to let him stay over? Was she destined to make impulsive decisions?

Apparently her only true expertise was investigating.

On the other hand, she had never been stalked before, never followed before. Contemplating what might have happened if Wes hadn't frightened the stranger off gnawed away at her. What if she had lost control of her gun? What if the man had succeeded in whatever he had planned?

It wasn't like her to be insecure. She could handle her own protection. Why had this been different? Because it was a first?

Giving up on sleep, she got out of bed and put on her long robe. Maybe some more chamomile would help.

Shortly before eleven, she cautiously stepped into the living room. Seeing Wes on his side facing the back of the couch, she went into the kitchen and started hot water going in a teapot.

"You couldn't sleep, either, huh?"

Indie jumped. She hadn't heard Wes get up, but there he stood, shirtless, with messy hair and sexy blue eyes. Taking in the vision of such gorgeousness explained to some extent why she'd agreed to let him stay. She had to stop doing that...

She breathed out, giving in to the truth. "No. I never invite strangers to sleep over."

"I never invite myself into a stranger's house," he said.

Oddly, that reassured her. Based on their brief interaction, it did seem like Wes was a man who kept to himself. He had stepped out of his comfort zone, just like her. The fact that he had insisted, pretty much, said the stalker had spooked him, too. That only added to her unease.

The teapot began to whistle. Indie took it off the heat.

"Besides, we aren't complete strangers," Wes said.

Yeah, sort of...

"You're safe with me," he added.

"That's just it. I can see to my own safety." She knew she sounded as frustrated as she felt.

"I meant…the other kind of safe. Me, man, you woman. That kind." He grinned, impossibly handsome.

He was going to test her willpower to do better in making decisions with men. She just knew it. He definitely seemed nice, but she didn't know him. Yet.

The next morning, after barely getting a wink of sleep, Wes found Indie to be again a sight for sore eyes. She'd gotten ready for the day as she emerged in the kitchen and saw Wes with a cup of coffee.

"Good morning." He handed her a cup. "Not sure how you take it."

"Black. Thanks."

He had checked outside numerous times and around 3:00 a.m. he'd seen a man walking along the side of the driveway. Wes had taken his gun and gone to stand on the front porch. The man had turned and walked back down the driveway. Wes had done nothing but think about Indie's safety after that, and he had come to a difficult decision.

"I saw him again last night," he told her.

Her head shot toward him. "What?" Her eyes were full of worry and also maybe a little anger.

"I went out on the front porch with my rifle and he turned and left," he said.

Indie sighed and ran her fingers through her long hair.

"I think you should come and stay at my ranch

until your investigation is over," he suggested grimly. "I have a den that also functions as a second office. The killer doesn't know me or where I live. You'll be safe there."

Indie sat at her table, put down her cup and stared into the dark liquid. "I'll admit, having a stalker who might be the killer I'm after is unsettling, but as I've mentioned before, I'm trained for this, Wes. You really don't have to worry about me."

"Then I can keep staying here. Call it being overprotective, but I don't want any other man doing that for you."

Indie glanced around her house. "You have a point that he doesn't know where you live."

He let her mull through it.

"Since you were at the engagement party, I assume you live near the Chelseys? Or know them?" she asked.

"I own the ranch next to theirs."

"I've never spent a lot of time on one before but they've always intrigued me," she said.

"I usually work all day, so I'd be out of your hair if you stay with me a while," he said. "And if you need to go into the city, I could go with you in case you need a little extra defense," he added, putting his hand to his heart.

She looked up at him and smiled slightly. "And here I thought you were the rough and tough type."

"Oh, I can be. But not in situations like this...or with a beautiful woman who likes ranches."

After a while, she finally said, "I'd rather you didn't stay in my house. I'll come and stay with you."

He wondered why but said, "Okay."

"I'll need to pack."

"I'll wait for you." Wes never did anything impulsive. Well, the last time he had, it had been to marry Charlotte. Maybe jumping into this was too hasty. He could tell himself he was doing this to make sure she was all right, but deep down he knew it was more than that.

Something about Indie had struck a chord with him the moment he saw her standing around at Julien's engagement party. He couldn't say he had felt the same spark the first time he had seen Charlotte.

Back then, he had been consumed with loneliness and tormented by memories of his first wife. This was different. And maybe that should put him in check. One thing he could not do was rush into something. He sensed by his conversation with Indie that she felt the same. Maybe that would be enough to keep things casual.

Indie couldn't believe she had agreed to stay with Wes, a man she had just met last night. She could have called the agency for backup and security, but something about Wes intrigued her. He didn't smile much and didn't seem to have any real sense of humor. He was also technically still married. But he clearly had a good heart despite his austere exterior. She had also done a background check on him and he had a sparkling clean record. Not even any speeding tickets.

She had been ultracareful on the drive to the ranch, ensuring they weren't followed. The lane leading to the ranch was long and beautiful, lined with trees and bushes bursting with late spring flowers.

The ranch house was big—at least to her, probably around five thousand square feet, a lot of space for one man. Wes's first wife had lived here, too, and maybe they had originally planned on making a family. She wondered what had happened there. Once upon a time she had looked forward to having a family of her own, but those dreams had been shattered. Perhaps permanently.

Made of big, earthy-colored stones, the house looked stately. Double front doors were inset and situated beneath a covered porch. Three-framed windows flanked that and the second story had a row of eight single-framed windows.

Wes carried her luggage into the house. She put her laptop case in the den.

"Let me show you to the guest room," Wes said, heading for the stairs.

She followed him to the second level, open to the living room and part of the kitchen at the top. She looked to her right and saw two doors on one side and a double door on the other. Wes went down the hall to their left. They passed a bathroom and he opened the double doors. She entered the biggest bedroom she had ever seen. It was a master suite with a sitting area by the front windows and a king-size bed. An open doorway led to a huge bathroom. Wes took her luggage into an enormous walk-in closet that could fit a bed. She had only seen pictures of closets like this. There was an island in the middle with drawers and shelving all around the perimeter. Some clothes were hanging on the racks but not many.

"Charlotte used this room before she left," Wes explained.

So they hadn't slept together. For how long? He'd clearly had a rocky marriage. Why else would his wife leave? Had it been something about him? Her gut told her no, but she no longer trusted that.

"Thanks."

He faced her. "I've got to go check on things."

"That's fine. I'll get settled and work a while in the den." A few awkward seconds passed where she was acutely aware of his tall frame and sexy blue eyes.

He nodded once. "All right, then. Then I'll see you around dinnertime."

"Okay."

He left the room without further ado, with Indie taking in his fine butt.

Indie busied herself getting settled in her room and then went down to the den, where she removed her laptop. Putting that on the desk, she sat and saw Wes had thoughtfully left the login to his Wi-Fi.

She studied the case file as she had numerous times already. Indie kept going back to Mya's ex-husband, Brad, and her ex-boyfriend, Todd. The ex-husband had an alibi. He was with his new girlfriend, Randi, all night, and according to the police report, the girlfriend had confirmed that. Todd, however, had no verifiable alibi. He claimed to have been home that night, and alone, but the report said he claimed to have no reason to harm Mya. Todd kept reiterating that she was a nice, good person and that he was devastated when he learned she was killed. The report noted this emotion was evident.

Still, Randi could have lied for Mya's ex-husband, and Todd could have been acting. They were worth another look. She'd start with the ex-husband's girlfriend.

Picking up the phone, she called the woman's cell number.

"Randi Howard?" Indie asked.

"Yes?"

"This is Indie Deboe. I'm a private investigator looking into the murder of Mya Berry. I know police have talked with you, but I wondered if I could have a few minutes with you to ask you some questions."

There was a long silence on the other end. "Wh-who hired you?"

"Mya's parents. Her murder case has gone cold."

"Oh. That's terrible." Randi sounded sincere.

"Are you still seeing Brad?" Indie asked.

"Y-yes."

"What do you know about his marriage with Mya?"

Randi didn't answer at first. "That it didn't last very long. Two years, I think he said. I thought Brad was ruled out as a suspect. He was with me the night Mya went missing," she said.

Indie supposed everyone would be nervous about an investigator digging into a murder case again. But

Randi seemed a little *too* antsy. She stuttered and seemed to take too long to respond.

"She divorced him because he was verbally and physically abusive," Indie said, hoping to shock the woman into telling the truth, whether she had already told it or not. "He was arrested on domestic disturbance, but the charges were dropped."

"What?"

Clearly Brad hadn't told her that. "Not something a guy like Brad would divulge to his new girlfriend."

"Is there proof of that?" Randi asked.

"Yes. You can do a background check on him, which I would highly recommend. I would also caution you about being in a relationship with someone like that. He needs help before he's fit to be with anyone right now."

Randi didn't say anything at first. "He hasn't treated me like that."

"Does he get jealous easily?" Indie prodded.

"Easily? I… I don't know."

"How is he with you going out with friends?"

"I have friends!" Randi snapped.

She was awfully defensive. "Has he ever hit you?"

"I'm not the one being investigated, am I?" Randi asked.

"No, of course not. Were you with him the night Mya was killed?" Indie asked.

Another long silence passed. "Yes. I didn't lie about that. I wouldn't lie for anyone in a situation like that."

Again, she sounded sincere. Indie decided to take

Brad off the top of her person-of-interest list. She thanked Randi and ended the call. Then dialed Mya's ex-boyfriend, but no one answered. Next, she tried the deceased's closest friend and she didn't answer, either. From there, she dug deep into all of their backgrounds. Other than Mya's ex-boyfriend, Todd, everyone checked out.

Rubbing her neck, she glanced around and realized it was getting dark. Her stomach growled.

She got up and went for the kitchen to get something to drink and see what Wes had in the way of dinner. On her way, she caught sight of some pictures on a built-in bookshelf in the living room. Going there, she saw one that looked old. A man, woman and boy stood on a beach somewhere. That must be Wes. Looking at the other photos, she found no others with his mother. There were three of just him and his dad when Wes must have been a teenager. She came across two of his wedding. He hadn't cleared them away yet, apparently.

Hearing the front door open and close, she turned to see Wes appear from the entry. He looked windblown and dusty.

"Hi," she said.

He glanced at the photos and then her. "Hi."

A moment passed as their gazes met, the energy between them heating.

"I was about to see what you had for dinner," she said, breaking the trance first.

"I took some lasagna out of the freezer yesterday."

"I like lasagna." She started for the kitchen. "I'll heat it up while you get cleaned up."

"Yeah. I need a shower. Be right back down." He left and Indie stepped into the kitchen and opened the refrigerator. Starting the oven, she put the cold pan inside. Then, taking a bottle of water with her, she returned to the living room and clicked on the television. She found a news program.

"Still no information leading to the murder of Mya Berry, mother of a four-year-old who worked at Schmidt's Bar and Grill."

Indie's attention was piqued.

"Correspondent Nate Miller spoke with Berry's parents. Nate?"

The screen shifted to a reporter standing in front of Mya's parents' house. "It's been almost a year since Mya Berry was found dead in a city park and still no suspects. Mary and Robert Berry have taken matters into their own hands by hiring an elite private investigations agency, Dark Alley Investigations. Every detective employed by this agency has a stellar reputation. The one assigned to this case is no exception. Indiana Deboe started her career as a police officer and quickly rose in ranks to detective. She has no unsolved cases and was handpicked by the founder, Kadin Tandy, a few years ago. If I were the killer, I'd be very worried. Cynthia?"

The news went back to the main anchors.

Indie felt a flood of dread flow through her. Great. Now the news was announcing to everyone that she was on the case. Not to mention the last comment would surely anger the killer even more. If it had in fact been the killer who followed her. She had checked her doorbell camera and that had shown nothing identifiable. She'd asked her neighbors and they said nothing showed up on theirs, either.

Hearing Wes enter the room, she turned the channel to a movie.

"They're broadcasting Mya's case now?" Wes asked, coming to sit beside her.

"Again. News coverage was heavy right after the murder, then quieted down when it went cold."

"Kadin handpicked you?" Wes asked. "Sounds impressive."

"He handpicks most of the detectives who work for him."

"How did he find out about you?"

That she would rather not get into. "Someone from the Irving satellite office told him about me." Told him about her family tragedy and how she'd zealously pursued a career in criminal justice. Kadin liked detectives with motive and passion, and she had both in spades, having lost her family to murder.

"Told them what?"

"My GPA in college. My case history." She had trouble talking about that part of her past. The rawness had never really gone away.

He looked at her as though he knew she was being deliberately vague.

To change the subject she stood and went to the bookshelf. "I saw these earlier."

Wes stood and came to stand beside her. "Yeah."

He picked up the wedding pictures. "Time to get rid of these."

"The others look old. You were just a kid."

He looked at them for several seconds. "Yeah. That's all I have...old pictures of my parents. My mother died when I was a teenager and my dad passed away before I left the air force."

She turned her head toward him. He had lost both his parents, too?

"That must have been so hard for you as a teenager, losing your mother. How did she die?"

"Cancer."

"And your dad?"

"He died by suicide."

How awful. He had been young, just like her, when tragedy struck. Her heart went out to him.

"He was devastated after Mom died. He never got over her death. Finally couldn't take it anymore."

That was so selfish of him. What about his son? What Wes must have gone through.

She didn't know what to say. *I'm sorry* was so overused. "No wonder you live such a lonely life."

He cocked his head and grinned crookedly. "What?"

She smiled gently. "You heard me."

"You don't even know me. How do you know I live a lonely life?"

"It's a hunch. Nobody talked to you at the Chelseys' when you were standing by that cocktail table. Isn't that the whole point of having cocktail parties? To be social?"

"You've got me there. Thing is, most everyone at that party thought I'd murdered my wife when she left me and didn't tell anyone where she was going."

She drew her head back. "People thought you'd killed her?"

"Only because Skylar saw a man digging near her property line and what looked like a body wrapped in plastic lying on the ground, and one of her friends reported her missing."

"Wow."

"Yeah. Imagine my relief when my wife finally decided to tell law enforcement that she was at her parents' house in Maine." Sarcasm dripped from his tone.

Why would anybody do that? Maybe this was another point when a woman should walk the other way. Or run. Charlotte had really wanted to get away from him. Why? What was the whole story?

"Why did she leave without telling you?" Indie asked. "You said she didn't want you to know where she was. But why?"

"She was afraid I'd convince her to come back. She didn't like living on the ranch. That, and I suppose she never really loved me. I thought she did when I asked her to marry me, but maybe she was good at pretending until she couldn't anymore." A faraway look overcame him and he averted his gaze.

"You're starting to sound like me," she said before thinking. She did not want to reveal too much of her less-than-romantic past.

His gaze returned to her. "What do you mean?"

"Having a perception of people that isn't real," she said. "I've discovered I'm not as good at reading men as accurately as I need to be. It leads to heartbreak."

He grunted, sort of a cynical laugh. "Then we have that in common." He chuckled.

Indie did not find that funny, even sarcastically. They both had serious trust issues. But his levity touched her in a mysterious way. Aside from his good looks, something about him magnetized her. He wasn't a nerd or a businessman. He was all cowboy. Like a young Clint Eastwood, down to the dark hair.

As they looked at each other, the energy began to change. Fearing sexual chemistry—her weakness— she asked a question that had hovered in her mind. "Was Charlotte afraid of you?"

His brow went low. "Afraid of me how? I've never harmed any woman. We fought like any other regular couple. She said I intimidated her, though."

Looking at him, she could see why. He was a big man whose sense of humor needed jump-starting. But every now and then Indie did see glimpses of his lighter side, and he was a nice person. He had a gruff way about him, though, that many people would keep clear of. Not Indie. She liked men who were direct and didn't overdo friendliness. It made them honest. Good or bad.

"I can see why you intimidated her," she said.

"Oh? Why is that?" he asked.

Without conscious directing, she took in his powerful torso, arms and shoulders, and spent more time on his masculine face and piercing blue eyes.

"You're a big man, Wes, and you have a direct way about you. If the truth hurts, you don't shy away from it."

"I don't shy away. I avoid," he said. Shying away held weakness. Avoiding meant he made a choice. "Besides, how can you say that when you barely know me?"

She laughed ruefully. "That's part of my curse. I think I read people accurately, but in most cases, I'm wrong."

He smiled, in an appreciative way. "Maybe it's best if we wait and see if you're right or wrong."

Yes, Indie did need to practice restraint when it came to men she wanted to wrap her legs around. She didn't respond because she began to feel uncomfortable with how easy it was to talk with him.

"Don't worry," he said, "I'm nothing compared to your killer on the loose." Again, sarcastic.

Reminded of how close she had come to being hurt or killed, or whatever that creep had planned for her, Indie felt a flop in her stomach.

The fact that the murderer used a blindfold on the victim had troubled her from the beginning. Why had he done that? The cuts and bruises found on Mya she expected. The victim would have fought for her life with all her might, but the blindfold seemed to have served a purpose. Had he not intended to kill the young mother? Had he planned to let her go? Who was he and what made him kill?

* * *

One of the things Wes missed about Charlotte was having someone in the house with him, someone to share meals and have conversations. Over dinner, Indie had talked about her day. He had told her about his. It felt very natural being with her. That made him uneasy because she had been so vague about her family. She didn't talk much about herself at all. Just work.

"What you do is so different than what I do," she said as they finished cleaning up the kitchen. "It seems so calming, and yet, it must be such hard work."

"It's both. I'll take you out with me some day if you want," he said.

"I'd like that." She started the dishwasher. "What made you choose horse breeding?"

"The horses were my favorite part of spending summers on a ranch when I was growing up," he replied. "My grandparents had a cattle ranch, much like the Chelseys', but I didn't like that they were raised to be sent to slaughterhouses. I was never a hunter."

She looked at him. "You're an animal lover."

"Yes, but I'm not a vegetarian. I suppose that might make me a little bit of a hypocrite."

"I don't like the idea of animals being killed for food, either, but meat is the best source for certain minerals. And actually, I don't eat meat every day. I try to eat fish at least three times a week."

"I like fish. I love seafood."

"Me, too. I had to grow into seafood. That's not a kid food." She smiled.

Finding things he had in common with her disconcerted him for a moment. He'd rather not start having feelings for her. Her vagueness suggested she had something to hide. He had blind trust in his first wife. His second wife had been a different story. He hadn't figured out what happened there. About the only thing he was sure of was he hadn't chosen wisely with her. She had turned into a completely different woman than the one he married.

"I played with horses when I was a kid," Indie confided. "I wasn't a doll girl. I was a plastic horse girl, something of a tomboy."

A tomboy turned detective. Playing with horses instead of dolls made sense. "Have you ever ridden one?"

Her face sobered considerably. "My parents took me to a ranch that offered horseback rides a few times."

"That seems like a good memory," he said.

She looked at him, turning from the dishwasher to lean against the counter, facing him. Some of the somberness faded. "It is."

"When's the last time you went to visit them?"

After meeting his eyes a while, she said, "It's been a long time."

Before he could ask more, she pushed off the counter and walked away. "I'm going to turn in early tonight. It was a long day."

Wes watched her disappear up the stairs, curious

and wary at the same time. There was something she definitely wasn't saying. What had happened with her parents? Did she have some kind of falling out?

Why was he even interested? They had a connection, for sure, but his intention was only to do the good Samaritan part and keep her safe. He had long since filed for divorce and it would soon be finalized. The full impact of getting a divorce hadn't had time to blossom into its awful glory. He was in no state of mind to start something with a woman. Best for both of them if he didn't pursue her.

Still, aside from growing curiosity, he found Indie extremely attractive. Would he be able to stop himself from acting on what that could compel him to do?

Chapter 3

In the morning, Indie came down to find Wes finishing up quite the spread for breakfast. Scrambled eggs with a variety of vegetables mixed in, bacon he just took out of the oven, a great big pile of hash browns, and a bowl of melon and grapes.

"Wow. No dieting here," she said.

He grinned. "Breakfast is usually my biggest meal."

No doubt he burned everything off working. Indie covertly studied him as he handed her a plate. He wore a denim shirt and wrangler jeans with weathered cowboy boots. Continuing her perusal, she couldn't help noting how he towered over her five-seven form. His black hair was brushed smooth but wavy enough to have a bit of a messy look. And even in profile, his blue eyes glowed.

Heart fluttering, she dished up a small portion of the heavy food and went to the table.

He brought her a cup of coffee and orange juice along with the bowl of fruit. Then he sat adjacent to her with his own plate, which had about three times what she had on hers.

She ate slowly, taking some fruit after a few bites, still furtively watching him. He made no fuss over appearances. He ate hungrily but without spilling anything, his big hands dwarfing the fork. She noticed he didn't wear a ring and also that his ring finger was longer than his index finger. Indie couldn't remember how she knew this, but a longer ring finger might be a sign of virility, in that a man with a longer ring finger likely had bigger testes than a man with a longer index finger. That meant more sperm production.

Looking up, she saw he had caught her observation.

Indie rarely flushed, but she felt her face heat up just then. Popping a grape into her mouth, she focused on her plate. She couldn't remember the last time another person had made her feel so flustered. Probably not since she was a kid. She had learned to be independent at a very young age. She'd forged her own path and didn't care what others thought of her. And men never made her blush.

"How's the case coming along?" he asked.

She heard his attempt to ease her mind and thought

how absurd that was for her. Nonetheless, she welcomed a nonsexual topic.

"I spoke with Mya's ex-husband's girlfriend yesterday. She doesn't appear to be a suspect. I need to find a way to approach Mya's ex-boyfriend. He claims to have broken things off with her, but what if he's lying?"

"And he has no solid alibi," Wes mused. "Did police talk to everyone he knows?"

"Yes. I spent the entire day going over all the reports," she said. "They all confirmed he broke up with her. Mya's friends and family said the same. What was missing was more detail on why."

"I'm sure you'll get to the bottom of it."

Indie wasn't so sure. If all she was hinging on was an ex-boyfriend lying about why he ended the relationship, she had next to nothing. No wonder the case had gone cold with the police.

"How was the body found?" he asked.

"A hiker was taking a shortcut through the park and saw her in a sitting position against a tree."

"That would be something no one could get out of their mind," Wes said.

"I know I never will. Some cases stick with me more than others and this is one of them."

"Because of her position?"

It was so many things. "She was so young. She had a child. And yes, the way she was left tells me clearly she was moved after she was killed. There was matted-down grass with indications of blood pooling in an area not where her body was found. And that blindfold…" Crime scenes always affected Indie. They were often gruesome and the presence of a lost life hung in the atmosphere. There once had been a person with thoughts and feelings, a daily routine and people surrounding him or her. But Indie was no stranger to that kind of loss, and that was what drove her to be the best she could, to bring ugly, evil people to justice and prevent them from harming anyone else. That was what got her through the horrors of crime scenes.

"Why would a murderer blindfold someone he planned on killing anyway?"

She no longer wondered whether the man had not intended on killing her. "There can be many reasons. Maybe as a precaution in case the victim got away. Or perhaps he didn't like looking into the victim's eyes when he killed them. Another possibility is that he did it as a tool for control. Serial killers have signatures like that. Some take souvenirs. The mind of a psychopath is a dark and dangerous place."

"You think this could be a serial killer?" Wes asked.

"If the ex-boyfriend checks out and there are no other persons of interest that Mya knew, then yes."

They finished their breakfast in companionable silence. Then Wes drank the rest of his coffee and stood, taking the plate to the sink.

"I'll clean up. It's the least I can do." Indie stood with her own plate.

"I'll take you up on that." He faced her with an unreadable face, looking at her a moment.

"Have a good day," she said.

He went to the kitchen island and picked up his cowboy hat. "You, too." With one more look he walked out the door.

What had just gone through his mind? Had habit nearly made him give her a kiss as a way of parting? Maybe he had done that with his wife. She did get the impression that he liked having someone here with him, which sort of went against his outward appearance of unapproachability.

Getting a fresh cup of coffee, she headed for the office to get to work. And to keep her thoughts from wandering back to the handsome cowboy.

Her case workload kept her busy for half the day. But then curiosity overcame her and she left the house to go explore, to see how Wes spent his days on the ranch, to meet a few people and pet some horses.

After about a ten-minute walk, she reached the first of four stables. There were other smaller outbuildings and one nearly as large as the stables. The big doors were open and she could see an assortment of equipment in there.

She had never been on a ranch like this before— a real, live, working ranch. She had gone horseback riding but had never been inside any barn.

Reaching the first and largest barn, she entered through the open double doors and saw two young men working. One was busy cleaning a stall and the other was in a tack room, putting things away. They both looked her way and stopped to stare.

"Hello." She held up a hand in a tentative wave, thinking maybe she shouldn't have interrupted. "I'm Indie Deboe. I'm staying here for a while."

"Who?" the man in the stall asked, stepping out into the wide space between stalls. About five-eleven and lanky, he wore dirty wranglers and a cowboy hat. "Are you staying at the big house?"

By "big house" she assumed he meant Wes's. "Yes. Wes invited me."

"Oh. He didn't tell us." The man held out his hand as he neared. "I'm Pete, and that's Phil. We're ranch hands here."

She took his hand for a shake, feeling the dirt and grime and withholding a grimace. "I'm an investigator working on a dangerous case. I'm here to keep a low profile, as it were."

"Ah, a PI. Huh." He nodded as though impressed.

His coworker approached, slightly shorter and heavier but in essentially the same cowboy attire. "What kind of case?" Thankfully, he didn't offer her his hand.

"Homicide," she said. "I can't really talk about it." Nor did she want to. She glanced around. "I've never been to a ranch like this. Wes said he breeds horses?"

"Yeah. Mostly quarter horses, but he's dabbled in Thoroughbreds," Pete said. "He doesn't believe in breeding spindly legs because they break too easily on the racetrack. He only breeds for sturdiness, so he doesn't sell a whole lot of those. He does get an occasional trainer here, though."

That sounded impressive. Wes must be keeping

his Thoroughbred breeding operation at a minimum until his line of horses showed profitable potential. She glanced around. The fine maintenance of the barn was evident. Everything was in its place, tidy and clean. There were many stalls and a few were occupied by content-looking horses.

"Why are there so many barns?" she asked. Did Wes have that many horses? She assumed so, but horses grazed and didn't spend all their time in a barn.

"This is the main barn for the working horses," Pete explained. "There's another one about this size for the stallions. They have their own paddocks since they don't get as much turnout as the mares do."

Indie wondered why. "Their only job is breeding?" she asked him. "Why not give them more time to run?"

"They're extremely high-strung. And it isn't good for them to be in sight of the mares. We need to control the breeding."

"Wes gives them more turnout than most ranchers do," Phil added. "He's a proponent for natural operations whenever possible. The stallions get a lot of free time. And exercise. Keeps them healthy in both body and mind. We have many different breeds. I sell them."

For a rough-around-the-edges man, Wes sure seemed to have a big soft side. Indie fought the surge of attraction that strengthened just then.

"The mares need a lot more than the stallions because sunlight promotes ovulation," Phil went on to say. "Wes has a lot of land to support that. His ranch isn't as grand as the Chelseys' but he owns almost twice the amount of acreage."

Indie heard his tremendous respect for his boss in his tone and saw it in his eyes. Wes's workers really liked him.

"Wes wants them to be outside as much as possible," Pete said. "Breeding season is underway now and will continue through July."

"Wes likes to keep it natural. He doesn't believe in artificial lighting to induce ovulation," Phil said.

"Are the other barns for foaling?" she asked.

"There are two barns for foaling. One is for clients who bring their mares in for breeding and the other is for our mares. They need to be separated to control the spread of disease," Pete said.

"Then there's a barn for the mares with foals and another for the stallions. That one is away from these to keep the mares out of sight of the stallions."

This all sounded so sexual. Stallions were hornier than human men, apparently. She smiled. "How do they breed? Do you turn them out together?"

Phil laughed a little. "No. Breeding has to be controlled to get the desired result in a foal. There's a breeding shed you probably haven't seen yet."

"Oh…" That would be interesting to see.

"Pete and I maintain this barn and there are crews that run each of the others," Phil said. "Wes has an overnight worker for each in case something goes wrong." He glanced up and Indie followed his gaze to a loft that had a small, enclosed room on one side.

"They sleep up there. He's very watchful of his horses. He cares a lot for their welfare."

Wes probably cared more about his horses than he did people. She was beginning to understand why Charlotte might have left him. She likely hadn't felt very loved. Note of caution for Indie. She did not want or need another relationship where the man didn't care about her.

"He also has a team whose only responsibility is hygiene," Pete said. "Phil and I and those assigned to other barns take care of the basics—cleaning stalls and tending to the horses—but that team disinfects the barns and the washing facility."

"Washing facility?" She hadn't noticed that on her way here.

"Where the horses are cleaned," Phil explained. "They also monitor for condensation. The barns need to be well ventilated and free of dust as much as possible."

The whole concept of controlled breeding fascinated her. The man running this incredible operation fascinated her even more. What had drawn him to this line of work?

Indie walked over to one of the horses. A dark bay with a gleaming coat, her eyes held a regal and confident look. Indie felt the animal observe her. She reached up and ran her hand over the soft fur of her cheek.

"You have it made here, don't you," she crooned.

The mare nickered softly and bobbed her head a few times as though to nod in agreement.

Indie laughed, enchanted.

Turning from the horse, she saw Phil and Pete watching in amusement. "Thank you for the tutorial. Is it all right if I visit the other barns?"

"Sure. Wes won't mind," Pete said. "He never liked it that Charlotte took no interest in his horses."

That was an odd thing to say. Did he mean Wes might be interested in her romantically?

Deciding not to dwell on that too long, she left the barn and headed to the next one.

Wes stopped his horse when he spotted Indie going into one of the broodmare barns. What was she doing? Had she reached a block in her investigation? Or had curiosity brought her out into the workings of his ranch? He found the notion intriguing and had to put a plug on his initial reaction.

How many times had he wished Charlotte had shown even an inkling of interest in his passion?

He waited several minutes before she emerged from the barn, smiling big and waving to one of the ranch hands in charge. She walked to the one that housed the stallions and was so immersed in her surroundings she didn't notice him sitting on his horse. A tree partially blocked her view of him and he was far enough away not to be conspicuous.

When she entered the stallion barn, he urged Gru forward, too curious not to go and see her engage with the workers there. Was she interested in the horses or the ranch as a whole? Maybe he interested her and she wanted to know more about him. The ranch was a big part of who he was. She must know that. He dismounted and tied Gru to the fence post of a corral.

In the barn, he saw Indie walking along the stalls, looking at the horses as she passed. He tried not to notice the way her sexy, round butt filled out her jeans and his body tightened in response. Her head moved up and to each side, taking in every detail of the immaculate accommodations. Wes was a stickler for keeping the buildings well-maintained and clean. The stalls were constructed of wood, which was more forgiving than concrete. Not all stallions were high-strung. But most were during breeding season, and they needed a safe environment that promoted top health. He also had a large number of ranch hands assigned to the stallions' upkeep, especially to keep them looking good for potential clients interested in breeding their mares.

Staying by the entrance, he watched as Indie stopped before the Thoroughbred Gibraltar, Wes's most rambunctious and unruly stallion. Because he was so aggressive, Gibraltar was never turned out with other stallions. Wes pastured him with geldings. Gibraltar spent a lot of time in his stall, however, especially now, during breeding season. The stalls were sixteen-by-sixteen feet and each had their own spacious paddock. The fencing between stalls and paddocks were high but not so high that they couldn't socialize. Wes believed that too much isolation wasn't good for any horse. Some breeders separated their stock due to behavior issues. Wes figured that as long as they were safe from harm and properly trained for handling and manners, their natural instincts should be allowed to run free.

Gibraltar whinnied loud at the sight of the intruder. He walked to the door and stuck his head over, bright, lively eyes rolling to view Indie.

She laughed and said, "Hi, there, big fella."

Gibraltar was a big horse. At over seventeen hands, he also had the kind of conformation Wes favored: large and sturdy, with a great blend of bone and muscle, balance and athleticism. He could get mean, though, especially with strangers and those in whom he sensed apprehension or fear. Indie didn't seem afraid, so Wes hung back a bit longer.

Slowly she opened her palm and let the stallion smell her.

Gibraltar tried to nip her.

But she laughed softly again and tapped his nose. "You behave yourself. I'm a lady."

Gibraltar nickered.

Wes rarely saw him behave like that with strangers. Charlotte hated this horse. Gibraltar probably hated her more. Those two had a lasting mutual disrespect for each other. His ex had rarely come to the stable. Usually, Wes only saw her out here when she needed something and she was too impatient to wait.

"You gonna let me pet you?" Indie reached up again, putting her hand on his cheek and rubbing. "Your coat is magnificent. They must take really good care of you."

Gibraltar's eyes blinked like he'd just forgotten he was the fiercest stallion on the ranch. Wes felt like reprimanding him. *A pretty woman comes walking in and he turns to putty in her hand.*

"You're going to ruin him for breeding," Wes had to say.

Indie jumped back from the stall and looked back. Her quick movement made Gibraltar jerk his head up and prance around in his stall.

She faced Wes, who approached and stopped before her.

"He's my best stallion. Most people can't get within five feet of him, or I should say, most *don't want* to get within five feet of him."

She glanced at Gibraltar, who had returned to the stall door. "He seems pretty harmless to me."

"He let you close. He must like you." Or sensed something about her that made him respect her.

She folded her arms in teasing defiance. "How does that ruin him for breeding?"

"Stallions have harems in the wild. That means they want to be the leader. During breeding season they compete with each other and that can sometimes get violent. That's why we have to separate them. If they see a mare who's ready, they get uncontrollable. You see, they have sex drive. If they lose that they're no good to me."

"And because this one likes me and isn't trying to fight with me, he will?"

"Look at him, he's a total marshmallow." She turned to look at Gibraltar with soft, curious eyes. The horse was stretching his head as far as he could over the stall door, his head bobbing as though clamoring for more attention. "He's not acting like a stallion. He looks more like an eight-year-old's pet."

Indie laughed louder than the other times and went to Gibraltar. She touched his cheek again and then his neck.

"He's so beautiful," she murmured.

Wes saw Gibraltar's eyes blink again and rolled his own. "Stop it, Gib."

"Jib?" Indie said.

"Gibraltar. From the moment he was born I saw greatness in him."

"Like the Pillar of Hercules?"

"The one and only. Sturdy and strong."

Indie observed him curiously. "You love these animals, don't you? It's more than a livelihood to you."

"Yes." His heart warmed as it hadn't in he didn't even know how long. "Last year, one of his colts made it to the Kentucky Derby."

"You sound like a proud daddy."

"I am. I don't proclaim to be among the best racehorse breeders. In fact, it's not the main resource here, but Gib is a special horse to me. He's strong and beautiful. Too many horses die on tracks these days. Somebody needs to start a change. I saw the trend changing a few decades back. Long, spindly legs, racing at a very young age, and breeding for speed don't necessarily mean a sounder horse. Let me show you."

Wes went to get a halter and put it on Gibraltar. Then he opened the stall.

"Easy," he said to the horse as he began to get jittery. "It's not your breeding day."

Indie stayed back until Gib calmed. Wes walked him up the wide space between stalls and then back, stopping with Gibraltar's side facing Indie.

"He has great conformation." He ran his hand along the stallion's coat. "Shoulders, ribs, flank and rear are all strong and proportioned. He holds his head high and has spirit." Wes then smoothed his hand down the front leg. "See how muscular he is? And yet not too much to make him look bulky."

"No. He's truly magnificent."

Wes straightened. "And he runs like a dream. Graceful and fast."

"Has he ever raced?" she asked.

"No. Gib is mine."

"I'd love to ride him, but I'm afraid I'm not experienced enough for a creature like that."

"I could teach you." Wes didn't know why he said that. Spending time with her would be dangerous for his libido.

"Okay." Indie sounded excited.

"I'll put you on a gelding."

"Only if you ride him," she said.

He chuckled. "Come on. I'll show you around." Wes put the stallion back into this stall.

As Indie walked with him out of the barn, she said, "Phil and Pete already gave me the rundown on your ops here. Why there are so many barns and such. You manage a pretty tight ship around here from what I heard."

"Healthy horses keep the revenue up and my employees paid," he said.

So she had met Phil and Pete. Those two probably had the most insight into the state of his marriage. He wondered what they had told Indie.

"What have you seen so far?" he asked.

"Just the mare barn."

He took her to one of the foaling sheds. A client's mare had recently given birth to a chestnut quarter horse.

"Can I ask you something personal?" Indie queried as they walked.

Damn Phil and Pete. "Sure."

"If Charlotte didn't like horses, what made you want to marry her? I mean, this seems like such a big part of who you are."

"I didn't know she didn't like horses. And it wasn't just horses. She wasn't an animal person at all. After my dog died she wouldn't let me get another. Remember I told you I met her shortly after my first wife died."

"Yes. That's so awful. How did she die?"

"Breast cancer. We didn't catch it in time."

Indie fell silent and he could feel her thinking he'd be trouble for her if they gave in to their attraction. He couldn't deny it. But he also could not make the same mistake again, falling for a woman so quickly only to discover later that it was a bad decision. He knew in his gut that he and Indie had the same kind of chemistry he and Charlotte had.

"Do you still love Charlotte?" Indie asked quietly.

Wes stopped walking in front of the foaling barn. "I've had some time to think about that." He looked away from her pretty face at the rolling hills in the distance, and squinted under the bright spring sun. "Truth is, I thought I loved her, but she was more of a companion to me." He looked at Indie again. "That's what I had such a hard time letting go of. Contrary to what many think of me, I don't like living alone."

Indie's head cocked slightly to the side as she contemplated him. "The first time I saw you, I thought you looked like a man who preferred to be left alone. But now I think it's the way you hold yourself...your demeanor that throws people off."

He smiled. She made him feel so good. And she was right. "I'm not much of a social guy."

"You don't have to be as long as your intentions are noble, and I believe they are." She glanced around. "If the way you take care of everything and everyone here is any indication."

When she faced him again, her smiling, pretty blue eyes captivated him. There must be so much more to this woman than he knew so far. She had to be intelligent to work for an elite PI agency. But there was more, deep down. Integrity. Kindness but not so much that she'd sacrifice her principles to please others. She seemed forthright and he liked that. A lot.

But Charlotte had given him that impression, too, and look where that had gotten him.

Wes started walking again, opening the barn door. He called it a shed because it was so much smaller than the other barns.

"I'm sorry. I didn't mean to get so personal," Indie said. "I barely know you."

"It's okay. You're about to meet someone who will take both our minds off that."

She smiled and entered the barn. Wes took her to the stall where mother and foal stood.

The tiny colt's long legs bowed but he was getting around a lot better now that he was a few days old. Seeing them, he moved closer to his mother, who took no notice, as she was familiar with people. He blinked his eyes slowly as though sleepy.

"Oh, how adorable!" Indie gushed, folding her arm over the top of the stall door.

The colt had a rich chestnut coat, four white socks and a blaze going down his head.

"He's going to be a great-looking baby," he said. "My client is very pleased."

"That's good for business." She admired the foal a while longer.

That gave Wes time to just look at her. Her profile, with her long, silky blond hair draping down over her shoulder. She dressed casually but businesslike in tan pants and a long-sleeved blue blouse. Minimal jewelry. A smartwatch, earrings and a silver necklace with two hearts linked together. He wondered what that signified to her.

When he lifted his eyes, he saw she'd turned to look at him and caught him staring.

Time to get back to work.

"Well…feel free to make yourself at home here," he said. "You can come to the barns at any time."

"Right. I should get back to work myself."

She sounded as awkward as he felt. Yes, best they both get away from each other. Thank goodness his ranching kept him extremely busy.

She smiled and leaned back in the passenger seat that
seemed even more plush and comfortable now, and with
none of her usual distractions to keep her occupied.

Chapter 4

On a quiet street about a fifteen-minute drive from downtown Irving, Texas, Indie walked into DAI's Texas satellite office later that afternoon. Kadin liked to lease charming older buildings because he believed ambience improved morale and lessened the grimness of what they all did for a living. The redbrick building with white trim used to be a hardware store. The floors were still polished concrete, but the interior had been renovated into an open office space with modern decor in earth tones and splashes of color here and there.

Indie said hello to the receptionist and walked into a small area of cubicles. The perimeter was lined with offices and two conference rooms. Administrative staff worked away at their desks and she could see the other detectives had begun to gather in the biggest conference room.

She stopped at her office and put her purse down on the chair before heading back out toward the conference room. This meeting had been scheduled for a while. Wes had questioned her about going alone, but she was trained for dangerous situations, and besides, since Kadin was in town for a staff meeting, she couldn't miss it. He had taken some considerable convincing and she found his concern touching. She also looked forward to being with him tonight. She hadn't realized how much until she caught herself thinking about him on the way here. Recognizing he was an attractive man and that his ruggedness appealed to her was one thing, but acting on it and allowing something more to grow between them was something else entirely.

Julien was there and she took the seat next to him. Del Stone sat across from them and a dark-haired woman with striking green eyes walked in, taking the seat next to him.

Del glanced over and did a double take. She probably got that a lot.

Indie had never seen her before. New detective?

Just then Kadin Tandy strode in. A cowboy hat shaded his unflinching gray eyes and unruly black hair stuck out under the rim. He had presence like Wes McCann. Indie had always admired Kadin for his uncompromising dedication to justice. He had an intensity about him that she respected because it was directed exactly where she aimed. At the bad guys. The ones who ruined innocent lives. But she had never connected ruggedness to a man who attracted her.

"Hello, everyone," he said as he took his spot at the head of the table, not sitting, but putting his hands on the back of the chair and meeting everyone's eyes in a round of greeting.

"First, I would like to introduce you to our newest member of the team, Jacey Cruz. She'll be here temporarily until we can transfer her to our Calgary office. She's been with DAI for two years. Prior to her coming to us she was a US marshal and before that, just like many of us, a policeperson and detective. She's got a PhD in criminal justice." Kadin turned and offered an outstretched hand to her.

"Thank you." Jacey took his hand. "I'm glad to be here."

Indie found the whole thing bewildering. She had so many questions. Why a new detective? They weren't overwhelmed at this office. Why had this detective relocated to Texas? And why *this* agency? She couldn't explain why but she had a feeling there was much more going on here than a relocation.

"As my memo to the company said, I am visiting all of the offices for a general status update and to get some face time with all of you. What the memo didn't say is I'm also announcing a reorganization," Kadin said.

That alerted Indie. What kind of reorganization? No wonder the head of DAI had come here personally. The reorg must be big. He intended to visit all satellite offices personally.

"Don't worry… Dark Alley is still a full-force private investigations agency with the support of official law enforcement. We've worked hard over the years to nurture our professional relationship with police and FBI from all over the States." His eyes met all four of their gazes before he said, "But I want to take this organization to a new level. A Most Wanted level. As it happens, I have access to a televised network through one of our investigators. We can go live with our unsolved cases to seek out tips from the general public."

"You mean like…a call-in center?" Indie asked.

"Yes. Through Brycen Cage. I spoke with him about making his show more of a crime-stopping program. We're discussing the plan but we have his full support. In fact, he's pretty excited about the changes I've proposed. We'll select all of our unsolved murder and missing persons cases. I, of course, will place most of my attention on missing or murdered children."

Indie's heart went out to Kadin just then. His daughter had been kidnapped and killed long ago. That was why he'd founded Dark Alley Investigations.

"I'm visiting all my satellite offices to make this announcement and to provide an update on current caseloads. There will be some big changes at headquarters. We're stepping back from boots on the ground detective work and teaming up with Brycen and his television show."

"Will we be doing the same here?" Indie asked. She was made for detective work. She didn't have the ambition to be in the public eye.

"No, and not all of headquarters will be working to publicize criminal cases, but it's going to take up a lot of resources. It may seem like we solve all of our cases but the bigger DAI gets, the more cases go unsolved. We do make a significant impact in helping our local and federal law enforcement partners, but the fact remains that some cases have little to no leads or evidence. I don't like that and I intend to do something about it. I may call on you for support from time to time but you should stay focused on the work you're currently doing."

He looked from one to another in the room. "Any questions?"

Indie had none.

"If we have an interest in participating, can we?" Jacey asked.

Kadin turned to her. "Yes. If you want to get involved, contact my executive assistant for specifics."

Jacey nodded a few times, looking somber. Indie became even more curious about her.

"Any other questions?" Kadin asked.

"At what point do we decide to turn over our unsolved cases to the television program?" Julien asked.

"That's going to be decided on a case-by-case basis, beginning with a review board. If your case goes cold for more than a few months, get in contact with Brycen's show manager. I'll be sending out an email soon explaining process and procedure details.

That will include contact information for everyone working to run the program."

Julien nodded. "I've got a new case that might qualify. I'm still working on a few minor leads."

"Wait for my email and we can take it from there."

"Will do."

Kadin waited a few seconds more. When no one else had any questions, he said, "All right. On to a status report. I'm setting up a site so we can all stay connected and informed on current cases. I won't go over all the cases, just the top few." He cleared his throat, then dove right in.

Kadin went into a detailed presentation on each of the big cases. Two hours later he wrapped things up. He invited everyone for Happy Hour at a nearby restaurant. Indie declined. She wanted to get back to the ranch before dark.

As they all gathered their things, Indie grabbed her purse and walked with Jacey toward the exit.

"What brings you to Irving?" Indie asked.

Jacey glanced over at her briefly and looked ahead again. "I needed to get out of my hometown. A change, you know?"

Indie could understand that. "Yeah, I hear you. I'm from Great Falls, Montana. It was great for family life but it can get very cold there and I wanted to see other parts of the country." She didn't mention she had other reasons for leaving.

"I'm from Wyoming," Jacey said with a wry smile.

Indie laughed a little. "Good to meet you."

"You, too." Jacey pushed the door open and they headed separate ways.

Now Indie would return to Wes's ranch. They'd spend an evening together, preparing dinner, talking…and just being.

Indie realized she enjoyed spending time with him. Maybe too much.

It was dark and Indie wasn't home yet. Wes paced from the windows in his living room to the kitchen. This felt a lot like when Charlotte went missing. Except worse. He didn't remember being this agitated. He'd been worried, of course, but now he saw that he must have expected something like that from her. Wes hadn't admitted it at the time, but now it glared him in the face. Charlotte had never really loved him; he had just convinced himself she did. As for him? He had been devoted to her and wanted them to start a family. As he'd told Indie, he really didn't like living alone. Wasn't that why he invited her to work from his house? No, it was more than that. He was attracted to her. Had felt it as soon as he saw her at Julien and Skylar's engagement party. But how could that be? How could he care so much about someone he barely knew?

He had tried calling her several times. She didn't answer. He dialed DAI and got voice mail. Now he thought this was getting serious enough to escalate.

Finding Skylar's home number, he called. Julien was staying there. He answered on the third ring.

"Julien. Wes here. Indie hasn't come home yet and she isn't answering her cell."

"What?" Julien was immediately alert. "She told me she was staying with you. She didn't make it back?"

"No. I'm worried something's happened to her," Wes said.

"She was at the meeting today. I saw her and another detective leave the building, but I didn't see her get into her car. Did you try her house?"

"Yes."

Julien cursed. "All right. Meet me at the DAI office. I'll leave right now."

Wes jotted the address down and then ended the call. His heart began to race. What if something bad had happened to her? The killer might have been staking out the office, waiting for her to show up. He must have known she would have to at some point.

All the way to DAI, Wes had cold sweats. He kept imagining that dead girl with a blindfold on, her face morphing into Indie's. Where was she? Not knowing tortured him.

Before reaching the office, he spotted Indie's car along the side of the road in a ditch. With his pulse climbing into this throat, he pulled over and hurried to the driver's side, seeing the rear end had received some dents and scratches. Were they there before she had vanished? The door was unlocked but closed. Judging by the angle of the car, it would have closed from gravity if she had gotten out by force or in a struggle. He checked the ignition and saw the keys were still there. Seeing her purse and phone on the passenger-side floor, he made a mental note to retrieve them. But first he searched the ground and found footprints. He followed them up the road until they ended with a cluster of several others. He made sure he stayed away from them to preserve the evidence for law enforcement.

Taking out his phone, he called Julien.

"I found her car," he said, hearing his own grim tone.

The other man cursed harsher than the first time they had talked.

"She was on her way home," Wes continued, fighting to remain calm. "It looks like she was run off the road and got stuck in a ditch. I found footprints, so my guess is she tried to get away but someone must have abducted her. There's no blood." That might be a good thing. She wasn't killed here.

"She said that the killer was stalking her," Julien said.

"Well, if the killer is the one who has her, she's in big trouble right now."

"Where exactly is her car? I'll get the police out there. Is her purse and phone in the car?"

"Yes. I spotted them right before I called you."

"Check to see if there are any calls or texts between the time she left DAI and when she got stuck."

"What about police?"

"I'll tell them you were there. It's okay."

Wes opened the passenger door and carefully took out the phone and found it unlocked. Some people didn't lock their phone. He navigated to her recent calls. There were none. No text messages, either. "There's nothing."

"What about her gun?" Julien asked. "We all carry one."

"There is none in her purse."

"That's where she keeps it. She must have at least tried to use it before being overpowered."

After returning her phone to the purse, Wes straightened and looked around, apprehension mounting in him. "There's a town just up the road. I'm going to see if anyone saw anything."

"Good thinking. I'll be working with the police and will let you know if we come up with anything."

"Thanks." While it was good to have a friend like Julien, that didn't help Indie when she needed it the most.

Wes hurried back to his truck and sped up the road, fearing the worst.

Indie woke groggily to a pounding head. She was lying on her back on a twin bed. The ceiling was dirty and had cobwebs. She tried to move her arm down from above her head but was stopped by handcuffs. Looking up, she saw she was connected to an iron-barred headboard. Everything that had happened since she left DAI came rushing back. Her breathing quickened along with her frantically beating heart.

She'd known she was being followed as soon as she left the parking lot. The car looked to be a black Charger. She'd taken out her pistol from her purse and readied to fire. First she'd tried to outrun him. She'd made it a few curves before the driver behind her rammed into the rear of her car. She'd swerved and the man behind her had rammed her again. In the midst of everything that was happening, she was able to home in on the fact that he had dark hair and wore a gray T-shirt. She couldn't see much else, other than that he wore sunglasses.

Tires squealing into the next turn, she'd driven as fast as she could, but his car was faster, and he'd run into her. This time she lost control, back end weaving left and right. She couldn't avoid driving onto the shoulder. Trying to get back on the road, she'd failed when her back tire got caught in a rut. She'd pressed on the brake pedal and rammed into a tree. Dazed from being struck by the airbag, she'd blinked her vision clear and seen in the rearview mirror that the other car had stopped behind her. She'd tried to start her engine but nothing happened. The front of the car had been crushed in, the hood bent.

Indie had opened her door and twisted to take aim and begin firing. The man had ducked down.

She'd waited, hoping someone would drive by on that lightly traveled road.

A few seconds later, he'd gotten out, moving slow and low. Indie had fired again. *Bang, bang, bang.* She missed.

He crouched behind the door. She didn't see a gun. He hadn't shot back at her yet.

His head began to rise over the edge of the door until she was sure he could see her. She took careful aim and fired three more times. He'd ducked, however, and she missed again.

Then he stood a little higher up. Getting out of her car, she'd fired at the same time she saw he wore a bulletproof vest. Her gun clicked blank. She had no more bullets. Pivoting, she ran up the road.

Hope soared when she saw a car approach. As the car neared, she'd begun waving her hands above her head. The female driver had seen her gun and sped past.

Indie inwardly swore and sprinted as fast as she could. She heard the man before he grabbed her shirt and tripped her at the same time. That was when she knew she was not dealing with someone inexperienced in the art of taking someone down.

Indie had fallen on the rough pavement, hurting her hands and knees and probably more than she was aware of at that moment. She'd tried to turn over and use her pistol to knock the man on the head, but he'd blocked her and punched her. Then he'd wrested the gun from her and hit her over the head.

Now, using her uncuffed hand, she felt the back of her head. There was a lump. She didn't think she would have been unconscious that long with a hit like that. The stranger must have used something else like chloroform to keep her out long enough to get her here—wherever that was.

Okay. She had to stay calm and focused. She had many years under her belt as a highly skilled law enforcement officer. Mentally going over the key parts of her training, Indie first began looking for something to get her out of the cuffs. She tested the headboard. It didn't look very sturdy. The bar moved a little when she applied pressure. She pulled as hard as she could and it slid partially out of the connection.

Encouraged and glancing at the door, which lucky for her was closed—for now—she moved to put her feet against the rod. Holding the cuff with her other hand, she gave the rod a hard kick and pulled the cuff chain with her hands. The rod bent and came loose. She slid out of the rod and scrambled off the bed, certain the man would be coming to the room any time with the loud noise.

She grabbed a lamp from a narrow dresser and ripped the shade off, intending to use the bulky base as a club.

Hearing the man approach, she went to the door and waited for him to open it. As soon as she saw enough of his head, she swung the lamp like a bat.

Clunk. Right against his forehead.

He jerked backward with the impact and fell into the hallway.

Indie wasted no time. She jumped over him and ran for the door. The hall opened to a small living room and kitchen area. She flung the front door open and ran for the road. It appeared to be a highway. It was dark and she had no idea where she was or how long she had been out.

Trees lined the road, so there must be a water source nearby. Slowing, she listened and heard water lapping a shore. She was near a lake. Looking one way up the highway and then the other, she saw a sign not far away. Hurrying there, she read Roger's Lake City was five miles up the road. She knew where she was now. Jogging, looking behind her every once in a while, she kept up a fast pace as long as she could, then had to walk.

A few minutes later she first heard and then saw lights that hadn't crested a hill yet. Indie ran for the cover of trees and hid behind one, waiting for the car to pass. It was the one parked in front of the cabin.

She trudged through the trees, fully expecting the stranger to be waiting for her in Roger's Lake. Searching. *For her.* She had to get somewhere safe and call for help.

Keeping to the trees, Indie walked a while and then jogged, ever watchful of the oncoming traffic. Car lights illuminated the horizon. As before, she darted behind a tree trunk and waited. The car passed. It wasn't the dark-haired stranger.

Running out into the road, she jumped and waved her hands high in the air, trying to catch the driver's attention. But they didn't stop.

Returning to the cover of the trees, she resumed her trek toward the town. The trees thinned and soon she was walking out in the open, the sound of grass swaying in a slight breeze her only companion other than her hammering heart and fast breaths. She had never felt this frightened before. Well, one other time, when she was thirteen, but that was different. She had to stop that train of thought. No distractions right now. She began jogging again.

At last, she saw streetlights ahead, and lights from

buildings. Reaching the edge of town, she began a careful lookout for the stranger's car. She had no idea what time it was, but it must be late because there was no traffic or people on the sidewalks. A small town like this shut down by nine or ten.

Seeing an all-night diner sign still lit up, she hurried there. On the edge of town with a large parking area and a couple of semis, it was likely one of the only stops a trucker could find a meal and rest for miles. Flooded with relief, she glanced around and went inside. A waitress looked at her, as did the two men sitting at different tables, one sipping coffee, the other fiddling with his phone.

"Please," she gasped frantically. "I need to call 911."

The waitress straightened from putting water on the phone guy's table, looking down and then up at Indie's appearance. Indie glanced down. Her jeans and shirt were dirty and she could imagine how her face and hair appeared. She also still had on the cuff.

"Are you all right?" the waitress asked, putting the pitcher of water she held down and going to her.

"I—I was kidnapped a-and I escaped." Indie searched for a phone.

The man with his mobile said, "I'm calling now." He put the phone to his ear.

Indie looked through the diner windows just as the stranger's car slowly passed, the dark-haired driver looking right at her.

Chapter 5

Wes's heart sank as he drove into Roger's Lake City on Main Street and saw two sheriff vehicles with lights flashing in front of a diner. They partially blocked the road. Stopping behind one, he turned the ignition off and got out of his truck.

He searched through the windows of the diner for Indie, finally spotting her sitting at a back table with two officers. Wes burst through the door and rushed to her. Other than looking a little disheveled, she seemed fine.

She saw him as he neared. Wes knelt on one knee. "Are you hurt?"

"No. I'm okay." She gave him a tremulous smile.

She must still be shaken up over what happened.

"A man ran her off the road and abducted her," the

sheriff said, a slightly overweight gray-haired man. "She just started telling us about it. I removed the handcuff from her wrist."

She'd been *handcuffed*? Wes wanted to find the man and strangle him.

In a shaky voice, Indie told him and the officers what happened and how she escaped.

"What did he look like?" the man next to the sheriff said, probably a deputy. Thinner and taller than the sheriff, he had a pen and pad ready.

"He had thick dark hair," she began.

"Long or short?" the deputy asked.

"Not long. Not super short, either. Maybe an inch and a half to two inches long?"

The deputy jotted down some notes.

"He was about five-eleven to six feet tall," Indie went on. "In good shape. Muscular but not beefy. More…lean."

"What about his face? Did you get a good look at him?"

"He wore sunglasses. I think he had an oval face with a long chin. Not too long, though. It's what made his face look oval. Normal-sized nose and lips. I'd say he was in his thirties. No gray hair."

"That's good," the sheriff said. "I'd like to get a sketch artist."

Indie nodded.

Wes had calmed now that he knew she was all right. His next thoughts turned to why he had reacted this way, so intensely. He didn't know what to do with those feelings, what to make of them. Ignore them for sure. It was way too soon to be having emotions like this. The timing was all wrong, in more ways than one.

But then, they did have a lot in common with their romantic backgrounds. What if she was someone he could trust?

"I can help with a sketch artist."

Wes looked up to find Julien standing there. He hadn't even heard him approach.

Rising, Wes shook his hand.

"Glad to see you're all right, Indie," Julien said.

"I got lucky."

"Luck might have played something of a role, but your training did most of it, I bet," Julien said.

Indie didn't respond. Her eyes lowered and she slouched like a defeated fighter. Her ordeal had obviously taken its toll on her. She had been abducted and nearly killed. What kind of impact would this traumatic incident have on her psyche? Wes didn't care. He would be there for her in any capacity she needed.

Despite everything, he was grateful for her training. Maybe any other woman, one not in law enforcement, wouldn't have gotten away.

"I'll arrange for a couple of security guards, too," Julien said. "I think it's best you keep staying at Wes's ranch."

Again, Indie nodded.

"Are we finished here?" Wes asked. He wanted to get her home.

"Yes, for now. When can you have that sketch to

us, Julien?" The sheriff pushed back his chair and stood, facing Julien.

"Tomorrow?" Julien looked at Indie, who nodded once more.

Wes had a lot of guns at his ranch. It was time to put them out where they'd be accessible. The killer didn't know where he lived but he wouldn't take any chances. Or could the assailant find out? Wes had driven his truck. If the man were smart, he could get a plate number and use that to track her down.

Wes offered Indie his hand and silently and without resistance, she took it. Julien noticed and glanced between the two of them but made no comment as Wes walked with her out the door. Now, to get her home safely.

Wes held her hand, opened the front door of his house and ushered her inside. He soothed her and made her feel safe. Protected. This was such a foreign feeling. She hadn't been with her family when they were being slaughtered. She had never been attacked. Vulnerability wasn't part of her agenda. Being kidnapped and cuffed to a bed, facing certain death had thrown her off course. Indie did not like feeling that way. It rushed her back in time to when she was a young teen and lost her family to tragedy.

Indie abruptly tamped down all thoughts on that time in her life, as she always did. Thinking about losing her family in such a horrific way pulled her down a dark hole. Like one she had just escaped tonight. She had been so alone after the murders and had struggled with anxiety for many years. It wasn't until she went to college for criminal justice that she overcame those issues. Law enforcement had given her a strong sense of purpose. It also helped her with survivor's remorse because she fought the evil that had taken her family every day.

"Do you want to talk about it?"

Startled, Indie jerked as she looked up at Wes, realizing she had come into the living room and sat on the couch with her legs curled beneath her. He held a steaming cup of tea.

She shook her head, wishing this debilitating feeling would go away.

"This is decaffeinated." Wes put the cup down on the side table next to her. "I figured you had enough stimulation for one day."

He made her smile saying that. "Thanks."

"Ah, she smiles." He grinned and sat next to her. "Why don't you come here. You look like you need a hug."

He opened his arm, indicating she should move close to him. He was already sitting close.

She hesitated.

"You need some TLC. Come on. It's not sexual. You need to be comforted."

After contemplating him and what he suggested, Indie gave in to the lure of human kindness. She scooted over to him, unable to remember the last time she had received this type of comfort. He wrapped his arm around her and she rested her head on his shoulder. Warmth and security washed through her.

She closed her eyes to the lovely sensation. He did make her feel safe.

"Just because you ran doesn't mean you failed," Wes said. "You're allowed to feel lousy after something like that."

Indie put her hand on his chest and let out a long, tension-relieving breath. "Thank you."

He moved his mouth and kissed the side of her forehead. "You're welcome."

She stayed against him for several minutes, until she began to feel stronger, fortified by Wes's embrace. At last, she lifted her head, feeling sleepy now.

"That's much better. You don't look like a scared rabbit anymore," he said.

She smiled softly, appreciating his direct honesty more than he could ever know, and his sense of humor—which, she realized, he had after all.

"Let's take your tea and fill a tub for you," he said.

She did feel grimy. And she needed to get out of these clothes. Maybe she'd throw them away.

Taking the cup of tea, she followed Wes upstairs. He filled the tub while she gathered a nightgown and then sat on the closed toilet seat, sipping tea. Once ready, Wes moved away and headed for the door.

"Holler if you need anything." He closed the door on his way out.

Indie undressed and climbed into the tub. Leaning back, she relaxed and tried to stop replays of waking to find herself at the mercy of a murderer. Wes's reassuring attention was short-lived. Maybe it would take time to get over what happened, but right now she wasn't ready to face the world. She did not like the fact that she had been so scared. After all, she had vowed to never allow criminals to scare her, as they had when she was a young teen. She would take them down. One by one. This man was no different. She had to keep telling herself that.

Except she couldn't. This stalker was like no other she had encountered. He had a cold and calculating way about him. The way he patiently kept watch on DAI, waiting for that one day when she'd go into the office. The way he had let her shoot at him until she ran out of bullets. The way he had driven past the diner and looked at her. All that calm. No feeling. No empathy. Just darkness.

She was convinced she was dealing with a serial killer. He had the behavioral profile. She bet he had the background to match. He'd most likely had an unsteady, dysfunctional childhood, possibly with parents who showed no love or affection and no real guidance, or maybe they were rarely around. Maybe he had even been abused physically or sexually. A child growing up exposed to trauma could become desensitized to the emotional response to trauma. He likely grew up never learning how to feel and developed a perception of emotions, or learned how to pretend to have them.

Finished with her bath, she dried off and put on her nightgown. Thinking about Mya's killer from a private investigator's point of view helped, but she still needed some company. She hoped Wes hadn't gone to bed yet.

She found him in his office, one door down from her bedroom. He turned when he must have heard her.

"All freshened up?" he asked.

"Yes." She walked into the room, noticing how he took in her nightgown. It was sleeveless and quite modest, with a high scoop neck and a hem that went to the top of her ankles.

She decided the best approach would be to be forthright. "I don't want to be alone tonight."

"Okay…" He didn't seem to follow.

"Are you going to bed soon?"

"Do you want me to stay up with you? I can."

She stopped a couple of feet from him. "Can I sleep with you? Just for tonight?"

He blinked. Once. Twice. And then stared at her.

"I—I don't mean like that," she said.

He seemed to shake himself back to reality. Pushing back his chair, he stood and faced her. "Of course not. I didn't take it like that. It's just… I wasn't expecting it. Yes, of course you can sleep with me tonight. Why don't you go get tucked in. I'll be in there in a few minutes."

"Okay." Relieved, she walked back down the hall, past the bathroom and her room, to Wes's masculine bedroom.

She was too tired to notice much other than the dark comforter and open walk-in closet. Then fleetingly wondered if he had changed the decor after Charlotte left.

She got into bed and relaxed. Hearing Wes enter and remove his shirt and pants, she felt warmth rush into her. Warmth from safety and coziness, like a co-coon, but also a glimmer of something else. Attrac-tion. But that didn't matter right now. What mattered most was that she get her mind back on track.

Wes lay down next to her. She had her back to him but just his presence calmed her. In the quiet room, she drifted instantly to sleep.

Wes let Indie sleep in the next morning, going about his usual business on the ranch. He hadn't stopped thinking about her, though. He would not have thought she had a vulnerable side. She was al-ways so strong and sure. That was one of the things that had drawn him to her, he now realized. But dis-covering other layers to her both intrigued and ap-pealed to him. Did her defenses have an impervious barrier? If so, why? What had put it there? Wes hadn't liked seeing her so upset and scared, but he did enjoy being able to give her what she needed, protect her when he knew she normally needed no protection.

After he finished all his necessary work, he went back to the ranch and drove Indie to the police station, where she gave the sketch artist a detailed descrip-tion of her assailant. She told the detective assigned to her case that she suspected the victim, Mya, was murdered by a serial killer. Because she had no evi-dence to support that, it was only a hunch. The detec-tive told her if she found anything to prove the theory to please let him know.

It was late afternoon by the time they made it back to the ranch. Indie then went into the den to work.

Hearing the front door open and close, Wes left the kitchen, where he had been contemplating what to have for dinner, and saw Charlotte walk into the house. Surprise could not describe his reaction. What was she doing here? Normally, seeing her gave him a rush of hope and maybe a little excitement. Now all he felt was annoyed. He still thought she was physically beautiful, with her long, wavy blond hair and blue eyes, but now that he knew what she was really all about, she was not at all attractive to him anymore. It was rather refreshing.

"I thought we agreed the house is mine," he said.

"Hello to you, too."

"What are you doing here, Charlotte?"

She came into the kitchen and stood before him. "I thought a lot about what you said right before I left."

He'd been in a completely different mindset back then. Wes had believed he loved her and their mutual love could be saved. He hadn't understood why or how she could walk out on him. Sure, she hated the ranch, but what about him?

"You were right. What we had together was bigger than this ranch. I admit, I'm no animal person, but we had a good life together."

Did she mean money? "Charlotte… I'm past this now."

"Past what?" Her brow scrunched in confusion.

Wes ran his fingers through his hair. There had been a time when he would have been elated that she'd had a change of heart. The trouble was, he didn't think she *had* had a change of heart, and he couldn't trust her. And ever since he met Indie, he had realized a lot of things about himself. Yes, he wanted a marriage and a family, but he would never have that with Charlotte. He could accept that now.

"I don't want to hurt you," he said, and almost added *the way you hurt me*.

Her mouth dropped open. "What? You said you loved me."

"I did," he said, feeling only a partial truth. "Especially before you cheated on me."

Her head lowered and she sighed as she looked at him again. "We talked about that. It was a mistake. A one-time mistake. It meant nothing."

It meant something to Wes, even more so now.

"I've only been gone a few months. I just needed some time apart to decide what I want, to be sure. You deserve that, Wes. And I came here to tell you I am sure now. I want you. And I want this." She opened her arms and looked up and around at the house.

"You weren't happy here. How can you expect me to believe that will ever change?" he asked. "I'm never leaving this ranch, Charlotte. And I want children."

He caught her blanch ever so slightly at the last.

"I can live here with you, Wes. And we can have a baby if you want."

"I want two or three kids."

She glanced away and then back at him. "You never told me that."

"Yes, I did. When we first met," he reminded her.

"I don't remember."

"You don't remember anything we discussed if you don't want it to happen."

She folded her arms. "Do you mean while we were fighting? That would be why. I never took what we said when we fought seriously."

It seemed to him that all they had done was fight.

"Will you at least think about it?" Charlotte asked. "I know it's sudden. And I don't blame you for not trusting me. But you have to believe me when I say I do love you, Wes. The ranch clouded my judgment. I've done a lot of thinking and I even went to a therapist. It was never you that drove me away."

"No, it was the ranch, which is a huge part of who I am. I can't change for you."

"I don't expect you to." She sighed long and deep, clearly frustrated. "I'm not explaining this very well. I love you and I can be here on the ranch because of that. I'll even ride a horse or do some work with you. Whatever it takes. Please, Wes. Just think it over. Do you really want to throw away our marriage? Because I don't. Of that much I am one hundred percent certain."

Wes heard her sincerity and appreciated that, but when he looked into the future, seeing her riding horses and cleaning stalls or feeding the horses, he knew what would happen. She'd be happy for a while and then she'd get tired of the ranch again.

"All right. I'll think about it," he said at last.

She smiled in a way he used to love.

Just then the den door opened and Indie emerged

into the hallway. She stopped short when she saw Charlotte.

Charlotte turned and saw her and then faced Wes again. "Who's this?"

"Indie Deboe. She's a private detective for DAI, the same agency Julien works for. Indie, this is my… soon to be ex-wife, Charlotte."

"Oh." Indie walked tentatively forward. "I didn't mean to interrupt. I was just going to get some water." She passed them and went to the refrigerator.

All the while Charlotte stared at Wes accusingly.

Indie retrieved a bottle of water and awkwardly walked by them, clearly catching the other woman's displeased look.

When the den door closed, Charlotte rounded on him. "What is she doing here?"

At her sharp tone, Wes knew she was jealous. And not in a flattering way.

"She's working a dangerous case and needs a place to stay until it's solved."

Charlotte put her hands on her hips. "Why is she *here,* Wes?"

"I met her at Julien and Skylar's engagement party. I saw a man follow her. He ended up kidnapping her and she managed to escape. She needs somewhere safe to stay and I offered her my place."

"We're still married."

"I filed for a divorce," he said.

"But we are still married," Charlotte insisted.

He did not like the way she threw that in his face.

As if she still had claim on him after everything she had put him through.

"Not for much longer."

"So you're just going to leap from being married to me into another relationship?" Charlotte asked, in not so nice a way.

"No. It isn't like that." But inside, his gut told him otherwise. Charlotte might be acting out of jealousy but she was right about what a mistake it would be to jump from a marriage into another romantic entanglement. That disturbed him, because he was starting to feel like he had no control over that.

"There's nothing going on between me and Indie," he insisted.

Charlotte didn't say anything for a moment. She just looked into his eyes before finally saying, "Maybe not right now, but eventually there will be. I know you. I can see you have feelings for her."

"No, I don't. I just met her… I hardly know her." That much was true.

"But you are attracted to her."

"What man wouldn't be?"

Charlotte nodded, her injurious look coming back. "Yes, she is exceptionally beautiful. And a detective, you said?"

"PI. But yes."

Charlotte took some time as though mulling that information over. "Does she like the ranch?"

"I haven't asked her." But he knew she did.

"Do the animals like her?"

Wes didn't respond. Why did she have to ask that question?

"They do." Charlotte cleared her throat and turned. "All right. I get it. I should go now."

"Charlotte." Wes went after her. "Why are you being like this? You wanted out of this marriage so bad that you ran away. You hid. You didn't want anyone to find you. Somebody filed a missing person report on you."

She pivoted at the front door. "I told you I needed time alone. Away from you. If I'd stayed in town, I knew you'd come after me and try to talk me into coming back. And I also knew you would have succeeded. That's why I didn't want you to know where I went, Wes." She shook her head, her eyes misting a little. No longer a jealous shrew, she had real hurt in her eyes. "I had my time to think, to be sure of what I want. And it's you. Please think about that before…" She turned to the closed den door and then looked at him again. "Before you do something that will seal our fate forever."

Wes would put it differently. He was at a crossroad. To him, his marriage was over, but which turn he took in his life depended on making smart decisions. Once, he would have taken Charlotte back with no question. He couldn't explain how, but meeting Indie had opened his mind to a future that did not include his wife. That said, his path forward was foggy right now. He had to remain solo until that cleared.

Charlotte studied him as he came to that realization. She knew him well and probably gleaned his thoughts.

"Okay," she said softly. "I'll go. For now." She opened the front door and left.

Wes tipped his head back and shut his eyes. Why did she have to do this to him? Charlotte had been an emotional roller-coaster ride ever since he met her. She would never stop.

Wes sighed. Deep down, he knew she was a good person, but she didn't mesh with him or his life in big, important ways. It confounded him how he had never realized that until now. Maybe he was just as tenacious as her. Nonetheless, he could not allow her back into his life. Now, what would he do about Indie?

Chapter 6

After Charlotte left, Indie wished she hadn't heard their conversation. She felt as though she had come between them, which was absurd because nothing was going on between her and Wes. Even while that was true, she couldn't deny the physical chemistry they had going. They just hadn't acted on it. Therein lay the rub. Indie had little confidence in resisting that chemistry. She was glad Wes had sounded so certain the marriage was over for him. What did that mean for her? For Wes? For the two of them as a man and a woman?

The house had fallen peculiarly silent. No longer able to concentrate on work, she opened the den door and peered out. The open entry was dark. No sound came from the main living area.

She stepped out of the den and walked quietly to the living room. Wes wasn't there. And he wasn't in the kitchen, either.

Where had he gone? She hadn't heard him leave the house, and given his protective nature, she doubted he would leave her here alone. Indie had never needed anyone to see to her safety, but Wes made her feel safe. And come to think of it, she had grown into adulthood fending for herself. She might as well have held a sword in her hand 24/7.

Putting those thoughts aside, she turned to the hall to the left of the living and dining area. She hadn't yet explored there. It was wide and dark, and low light emerged from one open French door. Should she bother him? The unexpected visit from his estranged wife had to have messed with him. Despite the inner voice that warned not to interfere, she stepped toward the light.

At the entry, she peered in. Wes sat on a leather chair, holding a tumbler of amber-colored alcohol. A low-wattage lamp on a side table shone on a bottle of whiskey.

He saw her the moment she appeared in the open doorway.

"I'm sorry." She immediately regretted indulging her impulse.

"No."

She turned back to him, intending to leave.

"Come in. I was just having a drink," he said. "Would you like one?"

"No, thank you." She went to the chair on the other

side of the table, wondering if he had turned to alcohol because he needed to unwind. "She must have really gotten to you."

"This is my second and last drink," he said. "And yes, she did get to me, but not in the way you might think."

In what way had she gotten to him, then? "You seem sure that you don't want her back in your life."

"I am sure." He sipped his drink and swallowed, then looked at her. "And her showing up here today reinforced that."

"How so?" What she wanted to ask was whether she had anything to do with it. Had their meeting opened his mind? Indie thought she felt the same, but it was too soon to depend on those initial feelings.

"Her lack of commitment to our marriage. All of our fighting. I think she believes she wants our marriage to work but it never does. She tries to hold it together but that fails. She always ends up unhappy about something. Living on a ranch. Me working long hours. Not being close to a city where she had things to do, like shopping and meeting her friends for lunch or happy hour." He released a long breath. "She was too much of a social person to settle down on a ranch like this. She might be hurt that I didn't fall into her lap again, as I have so many times before, but pretty soon she'll snap out of that funk and realize I was right."

"You must have known something wasn't right between you during your marriage," Indie said.

"Yes, but I had convinced myself I loved her and

all marriages take work." He grunted his incredu-
lity. "I was blind. She reminded me of my first wife
in a lot of ways when I first met her. I thought I got
lucky, but I wasn't."

Recalling that his first wife had died, she asked,
"How did you meet your first wife?"

"Online. We started chatting and eventually met
in person. We got married a year later."

"What was she like?" Losing a spouse was a big
deal. Did he have any lingering repercussions from
that? Marrying a woman who reminded him of her
didn't sound particularly healthy to Indie but she
barely knew him.

A soft smile shaped his mouth. "Warm. Funny.
Great with horses. Pretty in a country girl kind of
way."

"She sounds lovely." Indie smiled, but inwardly
thought he might be flawed in thinking he'd find love
if he kept looking to replace his first wife.

He would never see or speak to her again. She
knew that kind of loss all too well.

"How long were you married?" she asked.

"Two years," he said. "Two perfect years."

Did he realize he would never duplicate what he
had with his first wife? No woman would be able to
compete with that. *Perfection.* Many people martyred
those they lost. He said they were perfect years, but
had they been? She related to his tragedy, but she also
knew the mental toll it took on a person.

"What about you?" he asked.

Realizing he was asking about her marriage, Indie's defenses shot up. "I was so young." Lonely and desperate to have companionship. A family.

"How young?"

"Young enough to be stupid. I was twenty when we married. It lasted four years."

"And now you're thirty-one. Seven years is a long time. Have you met anyone since then?"

"I've dated a little. Not much." She sincerely hoped he would stop asking her questions. That was a painful part of her life. Not as painful as losing her entire family, but the universe could have been kinder to a young woman on such a difficult journey, fending for herself, not having a normal transition into adulthood. Alone. Always alone.

Now that she was older, she didn't feel alone. She felt in charge of her life, her own destiny. The universe didn't shape her anymore. She paved the way forward for herself. And she wasn't afraid.

Except now, that had all changed. She felt her control slipping, control over the predators she hunted, control over who she allowed into her life. Alone, she was master and commander. But because of her abduction…and because of Wes, her indestructible, structured life was shattering.

"I can see there's a reason for that."

Jolted out of her inner musings, Indie looked up at Wes. She had gotten lost in thought and revealed more than she intended—without even uttering a word.

"Well…" How should she respond to that? "I'm sure you can relate to what the end of a first marriage does to a person."

He grunted again. "Yeah. To say the least."

In that moment she felt connected to him like no other. Her marriage had completely different reasons for ending, but the departure had the same level of trauma.

"You didn't want the divorce?" he asked.

"I wanted a family," she answered simply.

"And he didn't," he said.

She didn't reply. There was so much more going on that had led to her escape from that monster.

"No. He wanted a puppet," she said. "So did his parents."

"Who were his parents?"

Oh no. Please don't keep probing. "Two people who didn't like me because I was independent and had my own thoughts about the world." Her tone was sharper than she intended.

Wes met her eyes without flinching. It was as though he understood her need for distance here and now.

"I'm sorry," he said, soft and low, wholly masculine.

Her heart melted. "Don't be. I just don't like talking about it."

"I can tell. You don't have to talk about it. Why don't we grab something to eat and go to bed? Just bed, I mean. And be together like we were last night."

He had a way of putting things so succinctly. "That sounds really good."

And it did. Too good.

* * *

When Wes woke the next morning, he felt a warm body curled next to him. Last night came flooding back. He moved his head just a little, enough to smell Indie's hair. Her cheek was against the curve of his neck, and her breath touched him at even intervals. She was still sound asleep. He stayed still, not welcoming the surge of protectiveness and...tenderness. The rush of affection. It was too soon for that.

Or was it?

Charlotte had been predictable.

Indie stirred, her body stretching alongside his. That had an immediate effect on him. He hardened. Her hand ran across his chest as she awakened slowly.

Oh, wow.

He moved so he could see her eyes blinking open, groggy, beautiful, sexy as hell. The moment of consciousness arrived and he witnessed her focus on him. Her eyes grew soft with recognition and she pressed her body against his.

Feeling her tense, he wrapped his arm more fully around her, his palm on her shoulder.

"Good morning," he said.

She smiled and relaxed. "Good morning."

Indie didn't seem to regret having moved this close to him any more than he did. Going on instinct, not wanting this sensation to end, he brought his lips to hers. He dropped a featherlight kiss on her mouth, but even that ignited a powerful reaction in him. With her indrawn breath, he knew she felt it, too.

Indie tipped her head, asking for more. He kissed

her harder and she parted her lips. When she put her hand on his chest, he rolled so he was partially on top of her. She slid her hand up into his hair, her other still curled at her side. Her nightgown was soft and thin, a light material that left little to his imagination.

When his urges compelled him to take this to a hotter level, his mind snapped into clarity. What was he doing? What were *they* doing? And *how* had this happened?

He lifted his head, wanting her more than he had ever wanted any woman. This was a startling realization.

Judging by the look on her face, she felt the same.

"Sorry." Wes crawled off her and stood.

She scrambled off the bed. "Must have been… waking up like that." She adjusted her nightgown as though needing more coverage.

"Yeah. Must have been." He found his jeans and put them on with his back to her, still hard.

"I'm going to my room."

"Okay. I'll make coffee." The idle talk helped. She rushed out of the room and he put on a shirt.

In the kitchen, his mind raced. His struggled didn't feel small. His entire world had just tilted off balance—not that it was balanced before. He still faced a messy divorce.

The feeling of her against him, waking, and then the explosive kiss kept running through him. He could not believe how good it had been. But he was in no place to engage like that with anyone right now.

It wasn't fair to her, either. He could not allow that to happen again.

The only question was, would that be possible? And what if he'd be making a mistake if he pushed her out of his life? If it was the real thing—something he hadn't had since his first wife—did he want to pass this up? Thinking of his wife, he couldn't recall having the intense chemistry he'd only just tasted with Indie. Yes, he had loved Rachel, and they had been good together. But it had been different. And that had him in a major conundrum. He needed time to sort through his thoughts and feelings—or maybe not face the feelings. This might be better stuffed somewhere dark and out of the way.

Indie regained control of her panic by the time she finished getting ready for the day. When she entered the kitchen, she didn't see Wes. He must have hurried to prepare for his day and left. Indie wasn't the kind of person to run from big issues. This qualified in her opinion. How in the world had she and Wes crashed into such fiery sexual desire? She didn't understand it. Waking up plastered against him certainly had been a catalyst, but…really?

To top that off, Indie was now über-cautious when it came to the men she dated. After her first marriage, a second mistake was out of the question. She never leaped into things. This felt like a giant leap.

She went into her office—well, not technically, and why had she just thought if it that way? She sat at her computer and knew she would not be able to concentrate.

Best to tackle the problem head-on.

She left the room and the house and headed for the stables, hoping to find Wes. In the stallions' stable, she found Pete, the ranch hand she'd met the other day, but not the man she was looking for.

"He's out in the south pasture," Pete said. "He should be back in a few hours."

A few hours. She couldn't wait that long. "I need to talk to him now. Can I take one of these horses and go find him?"

Pete stared at her a moment. "We've got a gelding you can ride. You can't take one of the stallions. They are too high-strung."

"Okay."

Pete went about saddling up a chestnut. "To get to the south pasture, follow the fence line road." He pointed to the far wall of the stable, indicating which way she should go. "You'll see the mares in the pasture."

"Okay. Thanks." She waited for him to finish with the horse, and then led the animal outside, where she mounted.

It brought back memories of her childhood and all the times she had gone horseback riding with her family. Joking with her sister, loving the sound of her young laugh. Her parents would talk and lean over to kiss. Indie hadn't realized it then, but they had really and truly loved each other. They had something special.

Indie listened to the clip-clop of the horse's hooves and breathed in the early summer air, clear blue sky above, tree leaves barely moving in a gentle breeze. It was really beautiful here. It took her mind off that kiss. *Almost.*

She crested a hill and right away spotted horses grazing. And Wes, off his horse, securing a gate. He must have moved them to another pasture. She was no expert on horse ranching, but she assumed over-grazing had to be an issue.

Indie rode toward him, seeing him look up as he turned from the gate. He stopped short.

Clearly he wanted to avoid her today. *Sorry, Wes. Not happening.* The ride had calmed her, but she still needed to talk to him.

As she neared, she noticed how he took in her form on the horse. And he took in more of the horse and her movement with the animal. Was he impressed that she had taken the initiative and ridden out to see him or was he involuntarily appreciating her as a woman?

She did a little noticing herself. Under the brim of his hat, his eyes glowed and his skin was slightly flushed from hard work. She refrained from looking too closely at the rest of him.

She halted her horse and dismounted.

Wes took the reins and secured the gelding next to his horse. Then he faced her.

"You took one of my horses to find me?" he asked gruffly.

Hearing a hint of satisfaction in his tone, she said,

"No. I had help from Pete. But don't blame him. I insisted." He liked it that she had ridden a horse out here.

"What brings you out?" He looked up at the sky and then back at her. "Something tells me it isn't the perfection of the day."

His eyes, shadowed beneath the rim of his cowboy hat, were amicable but beyond that unreadable.

She lowered her gaze to gather her wit and then met his again. "This morning... I..." She fell to a loss of words.

"I'd rather not talk about that. It happened and it shouldn't have."

It *shouldn't* have? She wondered. It had been so natural.

"I think the real point is neither of us is at a point in our lives to be entertaining romance."

"I couldn't agree more," he said, looking relieved.

She felt disappointment and grappled with that a moment. She should be glad he agreed with her. Instead, rejection toyed with her.

"If you were divorced and had time to get past that, then maybe..." Then maybe what? Impulsive decisions did not guarantee a lucky result.

"I know. You don't have to say that. I promise to be more careful."

"It's more than that, Wes. It's me, too. I don't normally do things like that."

"Like what? Kiss?"

"And sleep with men I don't really know."

"All we meant to do was sleep. You needed company, that's all."

Indie liked his easy rationale. She just feared her neediness had set off something else, something uncontrollable, but oh, so tempting.

"After my first marriage, I don't get involved with just anyone. I have to be sure. And this…" She gestured between him and her. "This does not feel certain."

"I agree. It's too soon."

She began to feel she'd forced him into repeating himself. He agreed: that kiss had been unexpected and the timing couldn't be worse. So why had she hunted him down and confronted him? Out of her own fears…

He began to look at her closer. "What happened in your first marriage?"

Inwardly recoiling from that question, she debated avoiding an answer. Something about him brought her guard down, though. Maybe it was his failing marriage. Did she have some kind of strange kinship going with him?

"Like you, I jumped into it too soon." She hadn't lost a spouse before that, but she had other reasons for being desperate.

"Things went sour after a couple of years?" he asked, moving a step closer. "You said you were young and stupid. Nobody can fault you for that."

As always her stomach churned when she talked about this or even thought about it too long. "I know." She couldn't bring herself to reveal anymore. Not about her ex-husband. "Loneliness drove me to him and into that marriage. I needed to be part of a family. At the time, any family would do."

"What about your family. Your relatives?"

Oh, boy. There was the other subject she always avoided. She averted her head, unable to look him in the eyes. "I don't have a family."

"No one? What happened to them?"

"I have some aunts and uncles and cousins but we were never close. They live somewhere on the East Coast," she said.

"And your parents?" he asked tentatively, as though he knew this was hard for her. "Sisters? Brothers?"

"Sister. My parents…they died." Indie wiped under her eye and breathed deep.

Later that night, Wes concluded two things. One, he was damn curious over what happened to Indie's family, and two, he was going to have a tough time disengaging with her. Part of him wished she would decide to take care of matters on her own and go home. Another wanted her never to leave. While he wasn't as stricken as he was this morning and had come to terms with it, he had to remain cautious. A dangerous killer had Indie in his sight. While she was a capable detective accustomed to dealing with these types, Wes would not stand aside and let her make her way on her own.

Their talk earlier in the day enlightened him on one huge clue. Her reluctance to get involved stemmed more from her tragic loss than it did from the technicalities of his divorce—or hers, for that matter. Being certain he did not want Charlotte back in his life had changed his whole outlook on the future. He was actually looking forward to starting over.

He would respect her need for distance. And he couldn't ignore that going from one relationship to another so quickly would not be wise. That didn't mean they couldn't be friends, though.

He finished preparing dinner. Lobster, steak and a salad. He had a bottle of red wine ready, too.

"How are you doing?" he asked. "I mean, with the abduction and all."

Indie's expression sobered. "I'm all right, I guess. It won't stop me from catching the killer."

Typical response from someone stoic like her. Hide the pain. He knew all about that. "No, but you're dealing with a serial killer." One who had murdered countless innocent women.

Indie said nothing. Just sipped wine.

"Have you ever had a case like this?" he asked.

Indie shook her head and looked at him. "This is the worst one I've ever worked."

Wes began to wonder about her real motivation for going after such dangerous criminals. Was this really what she wanted to do with her life? He didn't ask.

"It's a challenge, but I'll catch him," she said.

"I have no doubt," he said. "And I'm going to be with you all the way."

She angled her head, as though about to refuse him.

He held his hand up. "Nothing you can do to chase me away, Indie. At least, not until this is over."

She contemplated him. "You're a boy scout. You could have any woman you wanted."

Maybe he wanted her. "I'm not excessively wealthy but I do have some wealth. Sometimes I get the feeling women only want me for that."

"I'll bet the package helps," Indie said.

"The package?" he asked. What did she mean?

"You're not an unattractive man, Wes."

"Oh." He grunted a laugh. "You aren't, either. Unattractive, I mean." He watched Indie's eyes flit away and come back to him, a sign of being caught off guard. Indie was the least insecure woman he'd ever met—or she did a great job of beating it back. She was brave and strong. Intelligent. And beautiful. Someday he'd have to tell her that.

"Anyway…her declaration got me thinking. That wasn't the first time she had left and then came back. She was the most persuasive this time, but the point is, she's left me a number of times before, and I always wanted her back. I always took her back. I finally saw the pattern. Maybe I saw it before and just wasn't ready to face it. If I stay in that marriage, the pattern will continue. Neither of us will be happy." He paused because he needed the right words. "I've been falling out of love with her for years. I do need someone in my life and I want children. I want a family. I still have time for that. I don't need to settle for the Charlottes in the world."

He met Indie's eyes, looking closely so he wouldn't miss any sign of her reaction. She had none at first.

She met his gaze, strong and unflinching as he was finding was typical of her.

"No, you don't," she finally said, and then her eyes lowered to her glass of wine. She twirled it once and then again. At last she lifted her eyes. "Why did you tell me that?"

"Because I just came to a life-altering epiphany and my best friend isn't here," he murmured.

She smiled, big and genuine. Then she laughed a little. "Glad to be of service."

"I also think there's something worth exploring with you."

Her whole demeanor changed. She stiffened and her smile flattened. She shook her head. "No."

He held his hand up. "I'm not suggesting we rush into anything. I'm in no rush at all. I know I'm still married and that has to be taken care of. But I will say Charlotte and I should have divorced years ago." He had opened himself to her and she shut him out. He should sever all emotional ties with her. Now.

"Maybe it's a bad idea for me to have come here," she said.

The man in him would have nothing to do with leaving her out there on her own. He could hold back his feelings if it meant helping to keep her out of harm's way. "No. That psycho doesn't know where you are. You're safe here."

"I'm not safe anywhere."

"Don't go. You and I are on the same page. I can't get involved right now because I'm still married, and you have issues because of what happened to your family and, as a consequence, your first marriage."

As he spoke her mouth had fallen open. "What?"

"It's okay."

"What is okay? Why do you think you know me already?" She sounded offended.

Wes didn't respond at first. She was defensive, which pointed at her extreme determination to keep the past buried. He sensed she had never taken the time to address what losing her entire family had done to her. And that told him she had lost them at a young age. He knew because it had happened to him.

"How old were you?" he asked.

"What?"

"When you lost them. How old were you?" It would help her to talk about it. "Have you ever told anyone about it?"

Slapping her hand down on the table, she stood and walked away, going to the living room window, which was dark except where the outdoor lights shone on the patio.

Wes slowly approached her. He truly felt he could help her. But he had to push. A little. He wouldn't push too hard, though.

"I take that as a no," he said from right behind her.

She pivoted, startled that he had come so close. He must have stepped silently. She looked up at him with big eyes.

He put his hand on her upper arm. "You don't have to tell me, but I think it would be good if you did. I'm somebody who is unbiased because I'm just beginning to get to know you, and I have lost both my parents when I was young, just like you."

She didn't say anything, but she looked at him as though she contemplated doing as he suggested.

"Just spit it out in one short sentence," he encouraged.

She sent him a dubious look, glanced away as though to take time to think, and then met his eyes again. "My parents and younger sister were both murdered by my father's business partner when I was thirteen."

Whoa. That he had *not* expected. What a bomb. And she packed so much into one not-so-short sentence. Question after question popped into his head. He refrained.

"I'm so sorry," he said, then heard how minimal that sentiment was. "I know that's shallow and doesn't come close to comforting, but Indie…that's so terrible." No wonder she had issues. He began to think maybe he should stick to his rule not to get involved until well after his divorce was final.

"I could use a walk," she said, standing.

A little cool night air sounded good to him. And maybe she'd talk some more about her past. The more he knew the better he would be at making decisions where she was concerned.

Chapter 7

Wes's boots crunched on the dirt road along with Indie's sneakered feet. She wore a light jacket and her long blond hair flowed as she moved.

"What did your father do for a living?" he asked. That should be an easy way to get her talking some more.

"He owned a bakery in the town where I grew up in Montana. It was nice because he worked early and was always home for dinner. We did a lot together. Whether we stayed home and watched TV or read, played games or messed around in the yard, or went out, we were always together. That's what I remember most. And my dad thought it was important to take family vacations every year. We went to Disney World, camped and hiked and rode bikes." She glanced over at him. "And rode horses." She faced forward again. "Once we went to Hawaii. That was the last trip we took." She got a faraway look, forlorn and robbed of innocence.

"What happened?" he asked gently.

Without answering, she walked and stuffed her hands into her pocket, seeming agitated.

Wes gave her time. Opening up like this must be foreign to her. He sensed that in her.

"The business was good," she said at last. "My dad made a good living and did well with money. But it came out in the trial that his partner had spending habits that exceeded his limits. I didn't find out until I was older that my dad was in the process of getting out of the business to start something on his own. That was why his partner planned to kill him. If my dad died before he left the business, his partner would collect one-point-five million in insurance. Daven came to our house one night. During the trial, he testified he only planned to kill my father. But my mother and sister were there and saw him." Indie took her hand out of the pocket and wiped under one eye, as though brushing a nonexistent tear.

"I was at a sleepover," she continued in a strained voice. "When I arrived at home the next morning, there was crime scene tape and tons of police cars. I saw my mother or father—I don't know which one it was—being wheeled toward a coroner's vehicle in a white body bag. A policeman took me away."

That was so much more tragic than what Wes had endured. He imagined a thirteen-year-old discovering her entire family was dead and being whisked away into the bureaucracy of becoming a ward of the state. A world torn apart and a new, unfamiliar one starting that was full of terrifying unknowns for a young girl.

"I was placed into foster care," Indie said. "The couple were a little older than my parents and nice enough, but I was so alone. I didn't have my room anymore. I didn't have the nightly connection with my mom and dad and Evie. It was so quiet there and we never really did anything. But they were the ones who helped me deal with the murders. They explained what happened to my family, in a simple way. I probably got lucky having them to start out."

"How long were you with that family?

She released a quavering breath. "I was there for two years when my foster mom got sick with cancer and I was placed into another home. My foster dad didn't feel he could take on her care and mine at the same time. I stayed in the second home until I graduated from high school. I was never adopted. The older couple said they planned to adopt me but they didn't get the chance. Turns out they had other foster kids and did it for the stipend money. I couldn't get away fast enough."

Wes put his hand on her upper back and softly caressed to show some support.

She looked at him. "It wasn't until I was in college that I really started looking into my family's murder. Daven got life without the possibility of parole. Funny, how that doesn't seem like enough."

She went on in a broken voice. "I often wonder

why I was the one spared. Why were they killed that night? Why not some other night? I was normally at home with them. It just happened to be that one time I wasn't."

"I never question the ways of the universe. Sometimes I think there must be some reason to all of this and other times I think it just…is," he said. "We as biological beings, a product of this planet, have no way of understanding it all."

"It just is," she said, smiling sorrowfully. Then she stopped and faced him when he stopped with her. "I don't believe in coincidences. There was a reason I wasn't there that night."

Some cosmic, divine reason? "You weren't meant to die?" he asked.

"Yes, or I had more I was supposed to do before it was my time. Maybe I was spared to do what I do—solve crimes and give other families at least some semblance of closure."

"You definitely have purpose in what you do," he said.

"That's what got me past the survivor's guilt. That and a lot of therapy," she said. "It still didn't take away the loneliness."

"How did they catch the killer?" he asked.

"A neighbor saw him go into the house and then heard gunshots. He was arrested less than an hour after he did it."

"Why do people think they can get away with murder?"

"Some do."

He gave her a knowing look. "Not if you're on the case, I'll bet."

"I have solved all my cases so far, but some of them end up proving innocence before the real criminal is caught. It's important to me not to pin something on someone who is innocent."

"Noble of you."

She smiled a little and then sobered. "What about you? What happened to you when you lost your parents?"

They had a huge connection when it came to that. "I watched my mother fight cancer for over a year. She had a brain tumor. The radiation and chemo wore her down. Eventually she had another seizure and never regained consciousness. She went into a coma until the intracranial pressure on her brain stem stopped her breathing. I didn't learn this until I was much older, of course."

"How old were you when she passed?" she asked softly.

"Fourteen."

She met his eyes and they shared a silent understanding. He hadn't been uprooted from his home but he basically lost both parents when his mother died. His father had fallen into a dark, uncommunicative place.

"My dad was an engineer and worked long hours. I think just looking at me reminded him of what he lost."

"That's awful."

"When I joined the air force, he was fired from

his job. I didn't know it at the time but he was taking opioids, getting them illegally. Then when I first began flying fighter jets, I got a call from my dad's lawyer. I went home, planned his funeral and buried him." That was such a foggy time. He had gone through the motions in a bizarre haze.

"You must have felt as though you didn't have any parents since your mother died."

Just like her. "No, I didn't."

He met her eyes as she digested that. As the seconds passed, he felt them each thinking how hard it had been to be a teenager and have to fend for themselves. And, like him, up until now she had probably never met anyone else who could relate.

"Did you stay after your dad died?" she asked at last.

"I went back but got out of the service as soon as I could be honorably discharged. I bought this ranch with some of my inheritance money." He had been the beneficiary of both his mother and his father's life insurance, which, to his dad's credit, had been sizable.

"I inherited my parents' life insurance, too. And my father's policy on the bakery."

She didn't live like she had tons of money but she must. That was an enlightening piece of information.

"It was in trust until I turned eighteen," she said. "Luckily, my foster parents didn't figure out how to take it from me."

"Yeah, that's a very good thing," he murmured. "From the sound of it, life with them wasn't exactly a walk in the park."

"No. But in all honesty, I wasn't exactly easy to live with during that time. It wasn't until my senior year that I improved my grades and stopped getting into trouble. The reason I cleaned up my act was to get into college and get away from my foster parents. They weren't terrible people, but they didn't love me like my parents did."

After everything she'd been through, Wes could see how she would have relationship issues. He guessed she didn't trust easily, especially after being divorced. She may even have difficulty allowing herself to get close to anyone. It was a protective measure.

Wes looked around. It was a really pleasant evening. The stars were clearly visible, and the outdoor lights illuminated the stables. Nothing stirred. Even the horses were quiet.

"We should probably head back," Indie said.

"Yeah." It was starting to get late.

He walked beside her in companionable silence. Now that he knew her a little better, he found himself wanting to know more.

Once inside the house, they went up the stairs. In the hallway, Indie stopped at her bedroom door. No sleeping together tonight. He couldn't help being disappointed.

She turned to him, one hand on the open doorway. "Good night," she said with a soft smile that told him she had enjoyed their talk as much as he had. Not so much the topic, but having something that had been so difficult on them in common.

"Good night, Indie." He leaned over and kissed her cheek.

Her eyes widened slightly as she looked at him in surprise, but then that soft smile returned and she went into her room, closing the door.

Wes walked into his room, certain it would be a while before he would be able to fall asleep.

It was always hard to visit with family members of murder victims. Indie would never get used to that. She did have a natural compassion when communicating with them, though. She had gone through the same loss. Mya's parents had remained calm and motivated to help however they could. The police had already questioned them about their daughter's final days, of course, but Indie believed revisiting these details sometimes produced useful information.

DAI had two bodyguards that now tailed her everywhere she went. Wes had come with her for personal reasons, she assumed. He had waited with the guards while she spoke with Mya's parents. Now they headed for the victim's place of employment, where Indie would question her coworkers.

"How did it go in there?" Wes asked on the way.

"Her parents reiterated what they told the police. She went on a date after the breakup with her boyfriend. He was questioned and said neither he nor Mya made any plans to see each other again. No motive there. It looks random. The killer chose her for whatever reason." Once she eliminated everyone who knew Mya, she'd pursue the serial killer possibility in full force.

Arriving at Schmidt's Bar and Grill, Indie parked.

"The victim worked here?" he queried.

"Yes."

"I come here fairly regularly."

Indie looked at him for long seconds. "Really." He might be of some help, then. "Did you ever see Mya here?"

"I don't know. Do you have a picture? They showed one on TV but that didn't trigger anything for me."

Indie had a couple of different pictures. Getting out of Wes's truck, she retrieved her laptop case and dug out the digitally printed photos.

Wes took them. One was of Mya smiling with her daughter and the other was of her at work, where she posed with some coworkers.

"Yeah." He tapped the one of her at work. "I *have* seen her."

All of Indie's sensory antennas went on full alert. "Anything in particular stand out? Hair color? Height and build?"

"There was a guy who came in and talked to her. She didn't seem happy to see him. He had sandy-blond hair and I'd guess he was close to six feet with average build. He wore cowboy boots and a hat, but that isn't unusual around here."

"That's not what my abductor looked like," she said. It was a long shot but she'd check into the man's background. "The police report said his name was

Carl Brassard. They are looking for him. He works at an auto parts store."

"I'll wait out here with our new buddies." Wes gestured back to the other car, where the two body-guards got out.

"Okay. This shouldn't take long. Then maybe we can head over to the auto parts store."

"Sure."

She left him there, thinking he made quite a good partner. She glanced back with a smile, which he reciprocated with a sexy grin.

Inside the pub, the manager saw her. She had called ahead and arranged for the workers closest with Mya to be there. After greeting her, he showed her to a table.

The first waitress repeated what she had told the police, and said she never saw Mya with a man with blond hair and brown eyes. The second and third did the same. The fourth was the one closest with Mya. Indie had saved her for last.

"Hi, Colette. I'm Indie Deboe, PI."

"My manager told me," she said. A petite, brown-haired, green-eyed girl, she had an innocent and young face.

Colette repeated what she had said to the police. Yes, she was working the last day Mya had. No, she hadn't noticed anything unusual. Mya had talked about her ex-boyfriend prior to that day, how she didn't understand why he had broken up with her and that she wasn't going to date for a while. She was in good spirits her last day of life. She made good tips and said she was going to go home and order pizza.

The statement that she wasn't going to date for a while was new information. Indie jotted that down.

"Did Mya ever talk to you about a date she went on with a Carl Brassard?" Indie asked.

"The name doesn't sound familiar."

"He had blond hair and brown eyes. Average height and build."

Colette thought a moment. "There was one man who came in when Mya and I were working a late shift. We had both just got there. He asked to see Mya. She met him up at the bar. They exchanged words and then, after a while, Mya got frustrated and told him she didn't want to go out on another date."

This, again, was new information. "Did she tell you anything about him?"

"On our break I asked who he was and she said he was just somebody she went out with once but that she wasn't interested in seeing him again. She also said she knew him from high school and ran into him at the grocery store. That's when they decided to go out on a date."

Indie hadn't seen any background checks in the files the detective working the case had allowed her to see. She'd give him a call and ask if one had been done.

"Is that the only time you saw her with him?" Indie asked.

"Yes."

"Did Mya mention ever seeing or speaking to him after that?"

"No," the waitress answered.

"And when was that? When did she talk to him here?"

Colette thought a moment. "It was the Friday before she was killed."

"All right. Anything else you might have thought of since the police talked with you?"

"No. Sorry."

"No, don't be sorry. You've been a big help. Thank you." Indie stood. And reached her hand over for a shake. "Take care."

"I hope you find whoever did that to her," Colette said.

"That's my job." With a polite smile, she walked to the door and then outside.

Wes stood with the bodyguards, getting chummy, apparently. The three of them laughed at something, both of the guards keeping an eye on their surroundings. Wes's face sure looked handsome when he smiled like that. Rugged. Strong. *Unforgettable.*

"Carl Brassard came to see her at work and it was clear Mya didn't want to see him," she said to Wes.

"Possible motive?" he asked.

"With just that information, a weak one, but I found out Mya went to high school with him."

"Ah. Depending on their relationship and how well they knew each other…"

She was impressed with his astuteness. "And Carl's mental health. You're pretty good at this."

He chuckled. "You won't turn me into a detective just yet, my dear. Do you want to try and talk to Brassard today?"

"I'd like to do some background checking first."

"Then homeward bound we are." Wes glanced at the guards, who patiently waited to hear their next steps.

Indie's stomach still fluttering pleasurably from the way Wes had said "homeward bound." Home. Her home, too. She imagined living there permanently. While she had never contemplated such a thing before, she gave it some thought now. Living on a ranch had idyllic appeal. And maybe with Wes, even more.

"Is that you, Wes McCann?"

Indie turned to see a woman walking toward them, a man beside her.

"Catherine."

"You remember William?" She indicated the man beside her.

Wes's face hadn't lightened with delight at running into people he knew. Indie wondered what about them had him reticent.

"He owns the Rusty Lantern," Catherine said, sounding boastful over being on the arm of a prestigious man.

"I remember." Wes turned to the man. "William."

"Wes," the man all but sneered.

"Are those men with you?" Catherine asked, looking past Wes and Indie to the guards patiently waiting.

"This is Indie Deboe. She's a private detective and those men are with her."

"Ah." Catherine studied Indie as though measuring her up.

"Indie, Catherine and Charlotte are good friends," Wes said, then turned back to Catherine. "We need to get going. Nice to see you again."

With that he started for his truck. Indie followed, getting in the passenger side.

"What was that all about?" she asked.

"Catherine was always a showy kind of woman. She only made sure she said hello so she could flaunt her new boyfriend. As if I'd care." He began driving toward the ranch.

"William didn't seem too fond of you," Indie said, still curious.

"He tried to buy a horse from me about a year ago. I refused and he hasn't gotten over it," he said.

"Why did you refuse?"

"Well, like Catherine, he's showy. He wanted to buy a stallion when he had no other horses and had no experience with them. I told him he would have to choose a mare or a gelding and he'd have to buy at least two, since horses don't do so well alone. That wasn't exciting enough for him, so he walked away."

William wanted to be able to wow people when they learned he had a magnificent horse? People could be so shallow sometimes.

She watched the scenery whizzing by her window.

"Last I heard he did buy two horses from someone else and neither of them were stallions."

"At least he came to his senses."

"But not at the expense of his pride whenever he runs into me."

Indie could see why people perceived Wes as surly and standoffish. He was a matter-of-fact man. Reclusive by default because he rarely left his ranch. When it came to social finesse, he did not excel. It wasn't that he disliked social settings. He just didn't pretend to be someone he wasn't in order to appear friendly or congenial. In truth, he was friendly and congenial. Caring. And even a little sensitive.

She supposed few people saw that about him. She wondered if Charlotte ever had. Indie would venture to guess she was too worried about her own happiness to look that deep into someone else's character. Intuition told Indie that his soon-to-be ex-wife likely saw Wes as a masculine man, a cowboy and a provider. Since they had little in common, they probably didn't have much to say to each other. Why did Charlotte want him back, then? Security? She did seem rather indecisive. Would her resolve strengthen now that she had discovered Indie was staying with him? Some women tended to want a man more when another woman took interest.

Indie was not competitive over men, but something sparked inside of her at the thought of losing an opportunity with Wes. She did not welcome this, however. She would not get involved with a man who wasn't even divorced yet. Furthermore, she would not be *the other woman*.

Chapter 8

A few days later, Indie had the results from the background investigation DAI obtained for her. Carl Brassard had a criminal history. He had been arrested for assault seven years ago, and just two years ago had a restraining order issued against him for stalking. His father owned the auto parts store where he worked. Carl was married twice and twice divorced. No kids. Probably a good thing unless he straightened out his life.

Indie tried again to contact Mya's closest friend. Still no answer. Indie began to get suspicious. Was Hanna Foster avoiding her? How could she know her number? Maybe she didn't answer calls she didn't recognize. Still, Indie had left numerous messages and

Hanna had never called back. She knew her number now and could identify it and not answer.

Indie's next outing would be to talk to Carl and track Hanna down. Corner her so she'd have to speak with Indie. But right now she felt restless, with nothing to do.

The lure of exploring the ranch some more overcame her and she headed outside. She had to admit to being very curious about Wes. He intrigued her. Was he the straight shooter her instincts said he was?.

Yesterday she had seen the entrance to a one-lane dirt road near one of the stables. Indie decided to take a hike there. She had a new gun and some extra ammo with her.

Trees clustered heavier along the stream. Wes's ranch had lots of open space with hayfields, lush green pastures and outbuildings. Sunlight filtered through the canopy. She could hear the stream, the sound growing louder as she approached.

Ahead she saw a bridge. It looked old but maintained. It was wide enough to fit one car or truck. She imagined horses and buggies crossing to the other side. Stepping onto the dirt road again, she walked onward. A moment later, she heard pounding, like someone using a hammer. What was back here? The road and bridge were storybook charming.

Around a slight bend in the road, she came upon an old Victorian house in need of repair. The hammering came from within. The front door was open, as were windows, likely to air it out or keep it cool. Wes's truck was parked outside.

She hesitated, her feet slowing, but she kept going. An irresistible force drove her.

The steps creaked as she stepped up onto the porch. Just inside the doorway, she saw Wes in the kitchen. He stopped the swing of the hammer, a nail protruding from a stud.

"I was just taking a walk and saw this road." She pointed back behind her. Then she looked around the house. It had been gutted of everything but the walls. "What is this place?"

Wes put down the hammer and came to her with slow strides, sexy in dirty jeans and a white T-shirt. "It's the original homestead."

Indie looked around with new eyes. She loved things like this. Little pieces of real history.

"Who were they? Did you buy it from the family of the original homesteaders?" she asked.

"Yes. In the 1880s, Charles Eastman was a banker who invested in property. He gradually bought up acreage. Originally he had almost five hundred thousand acres but his sons and grandsons sold about two-thirds of it. His great-granddaughter had no taste for ranching and ended up selling.

"Mr. Eastman was an Irish immigrant who started out on the East Coast. Boston, I believe. He had a fascination with the West and decided to move to Texas. He read about ranching but had no experience, so when he arrived here and established himself, he met up with a man who grew up on a ranch but worked in finance like Charles."

"Who was he?" she asked.

"James something. I don't remember his last name. He was looking to partner with someone to start his own. He and Eastman met up and made a deal. Eastman invested most of the money and James ran the ranch. It was a perfect combination. Except for one thing," Wes said.

"Oh yeah…?" she said, taken in by the suspense.

"James was a womanizer, according to Lily. He had no wife, no kids. He was twenty-nine years old. His dream was this ranch. He named it the Double Diamond. Eastman let him run the business operationally but he did all the numbers. He was an investor."

"His descendant who sold must have filled you up with her history." She also must have been proud of her family heritage. Why let it go?

"Lily Eastman did," Wes said.

He'd apparently had quite a conversation with Lily. Indie had no affiliation with her father's bakery, so she could relate somewhat to that kind of thinking. But inheriting a ranch appealed to her more. She had never been interested in her father's bakery, and didn't even have that much of a sweet tooth.

"The Eastmans had old money Charles had inherited before he came to Texas."

Old money. "And he was successful in business?"

"Yes," Wes said. "He reminded me of my grandfather, who was devoted to his ranch and my grandmother for sixty-plus years."

"Seriously?" she said, thinking that this story was getting better and better. "Tell me more!"

Wes chuckled. "Come and join me out back." He took her hand and led her through the house.

She saw that he was in the process of moving the kitchen to the back of the house. The floors were already finished, along with the bones of a kitchen island and counters, but the appliances were still wrapped in heavy plastic. The herringbone-pattern wood floor was installed, as were the backsplash and walls of the kitchen. It was nearly complete. Indie was in awe.

The wonder continued as she arrived out on the back patio. While the yard wasn't fenced, wildflowers sprouted within border gardens near the house on either side of the patio.

Wes lit an outdoor heater and turned on the gas patio firepit.

"You've been busy," she said, taking a seat on a stone-backed, curved bench.

"I come here and work when I have time...and when I need to be alone."

"Oh." Had she interrupted? "Maybe I should go."

"No. I've been working for a while now. It's okay." He sat next to her.

"Charles owned the ranch outright and ran it successfully his entire life."

Up until Lily failed due to a lack of passion for what must have been her great-grandfather's dream.

"You got lucky, it would seem." His ranch had been in the Eastman family for more than a hundred years.

"I would like to pass this down to my children and for them to pass it down to theirs," Wes said.

Indie thought of how similar they were in that regard. Before she got married, having a family was one of her top wishes for her life. She hadn't had much luck with men and along the way had lost the ambition to keep trying. While she told herself she wasn't lonely and was happy with the way her life was, deep down she always felt that void. Something was missing, and getting to know Wes, talking about their family histories, brought it all bubbling up.

In all honesty, she hadn't thought about having a family of her own in a long time. Now, looking at Wes as he dreamed of a future that had yet to manifest itself, she found herself dreaming along with him. How many times before she got married had she fantasized about having a family? A real one. Full of love and laughter. Sure, there'd be tough times, too, but they'd weather those as a unit.

She had gotten close to realizing her dream after her divorce but that had ended just like her marriage. She didn't like thinking about Cole, her ex-husband. He was a liar and not at all who she'd thought he was.

"Do you want kids?" Wes asked, ending their long, comfortable silence.

"There was a time when that's all I wanted," she admitted.

"What happened to make you stop?"

"I don't know. I guess I just got too disillusioned. I stopped trying to find the right man."

He lifted a brow. "And if you did find the right man?"

"I don't know. I never gave it much thought after my marriage and another relationship ended."

"How many kids did you want?" he asked.

She smiled over at him. "Two or three. Girls and a boy, boys and girl, it doesn't matter."

"Three would be nice," he said. "It would fill up a house."

"Yeah." Love and laughter. A warm, cozy feeling filled her as it hadn't done since before her marriage.

Wes's eyes twinkled much like she was sure hers were. Then she began to realize that no other man had ever brought up kids with her. She fell into their locked gazes, into *him*, seeing him through the windows of his eyes. She had never seen them so transparent before, and truly felt his deep longing for a family. He rekindled her desires.

He moved his head closer, tentatively, keeping his eyes latched on hers. Indie didn't withdraw. She wasn't ready for this moment to end.

"I've never met anyone like you," he murmured.

"I've never met anyone like you, either," she answered, feeling the absolute truth in what they both had just said to each other.

He closed the space between them and kissed her. He pressed his mouth to hers, soft and gentle and full of meaning.

Indie placed her hand on his shoulder, the hard muscle revving up her passion. His manliness alone heated her body.

Sliding his hand to the side and then back of her head, he deepened the kiss. Indie had to breathe more air. Her heart beat faster. She heard and felt his stuttering breath and knew he was quickly careening out of control the same as her.

He slowly withdrew and looked into her eyes. Indie could stare into his for hours and not get tired of it.

"I want to make love to you," he rasped.

Oh, how she wanted that, too.

He kissed her again, this time harder and more urgently. Indie wouldn't be able to stop this, even though a tiny part of her brain attempted to. It felt too good.

It also began to remind her of her last catastrophe with a man.

"I thought I'd find you—"

The woman's voice cut short as she saw them.

Indie jerked back and covered her mouth with her hand, looking over at Charlotte. Mortified, she stood and rushed past the startled woman and into the house. Why did she keep allowing this to happen?

Irritated that Charlotte had appeared unannounced and Indie ran off like they'd been caught in an affair, Wes stood and rounded on his soon-to-be ex-wife.

"What are you doing here, Charlotte?" he demanded.

She blanched a little at his harsh tone. "I just came by to see if you'd had enough time to think things over, but it looks like you've made up your mind."

"You can't keep coming here. We're going to be divorced in two weeks." They'd already filed the petition and were just waiting for the divorce to become final with the court. In Texas there was a sixty-one-day waiting period—in case anyone changed their minds.

"Wes, we can still make this work," she said. "Why are you fooling around with that woman already? You barely know her. Are you just going to have a fling?"

"That's none of your business."

"It is, Wes. I want to make this marriage work."

"Well, I don't."

Charlotte didn't respond right away. But then she said, "Your judgment is just clouded by that woman. She's trying to take you from me. She won't last. It's a rebound relationship. You might think you're ready but you aren't."

"Indie isn't trying to take me from you." He hadn't realized how insecure Charlotte was and almost took pity on her. "I can't predict what happens in the future, but I am not your husband in any way that matters anymore."

"I admit we've had our problems, but I know we can work through them."

She was in major denial. He decided to be blunt. "Charlotte, I don't love you anymore."

She looked deflated. "I don't believe you."

"This marriage is not what you want," Wes said as gently as he could. "You've left so many times already. I don't understand why you suddenly want to hang on to something that obviously isn't working. I think you're having a difficult time letting go. Don't be afraid to start over. You won't have any trouble finding another man."

"I'm not afraid. I want you, Wes."

Her pleading began to make him feel sick. He couldn't believe he had fought so hard to keep this marriage alive. And after kissing Indie, he knew he had never had that kind of passion with Charlotte.

"I need you to leave and never come back, Charlotte," he said.

Tears sprung to her eyes and spilled over. "It's that woman. She's poisoned your thinking."

Wes shook his head. "She has nothing to do with my decision." But inwardly he wondered if that was true.

Charlotte wiped her cheeks.

"Please. Go. I don't want to see you here again," he said.

"It is her, Wes. There will come a day when you realize the timing isn't right to start over with someone new."

"Charlotte." He put a warning tone in his voice.

"I'm going." She turned. "I won't come back unless you say you want me to come home." She left.

Wes felt nothing but relief. At least he didn't have to worry about a stalker.

He drove back to his house to find Indie. He did not like how she'd run off as though she were breaking up a marriage. The den door was closed and he heard her typing on her computer. He knocked.

The typing stopped.

"Come in."

He opened the door and saw her looking at him warily.

"Sorry about that," he said. "She won't be back."

Indie cocked her head as though that meant little to her.

"My divorce is final in two weeks."

Her eyebrows rose.

"I don't love her," he said.

"That doesn't matter. Divorce is a huge, life-altering event. You can't just jump out of one marriage into a new relationship."

"Typically, that might be true. But I don't think there is anything typical about you and me."

Indie stood and walked to him. "Wes, we are not boyfriend and girlfriend."

"I know, but what harm is there in getting to know each other?" He actually couldn't believe he was pushing this. What was happening to him?

"Probably a lot of harm," she said. "I don't want my heart broken."

"I don't want that, either. But how are we going to know what this is if we don't let it run its course?"

"We shouldn't have talked about having children."

What did that have to do with them getting to know each other? So they both wanted kids. That didn't mean they'd start trying to make them right now.

"All right. I'll keep my distance from you until my divorce is final. Then you and I are going on a date." Before she could argue—and he knew she would—he turned and left, shutting the door behind him.

Chapter 9

Indie had her bodyguards, so she wasn't surprised Wes had done as he promised and kept his distance. She almost missed him. She saw him from time to time around the house. Rather than prepare dinners, he had them brought in and never ate with her. Many times Indie questioned the logic of continuing to stay here. The guards would go where she went. But for some reason she turned away from the idea of returning home. She loved this ranch. Everything about it. It brought back some of the best memories she had as a child and reminded her of her fondness for horses. The smell of hay. The sounds of their hooves and whinnies. The solitude, the peace and quiet. And Wes. *Especially Wes.* She had to be honest. He was what kept her from leaving. Aside from the complications keeping them apart right now, he brightened her world just by being near.

Top that off with the fact that his divorce was final yesterday. Nothing could pry her from here.

With her guards acting as chauffeurs, she rode in the back of their sedan to find Mya's friend Hanna. The driver, Samuel, had just pulled to a stop in front of a dental office where she worked as a hygienist. Thomas, the passenger, got out and opened the back door for her.

The driver stayed in the car while Thomas accompanied her into the dental office.

"We're here to speak with Hanna Foster," Indie said to the receptionist. She showed the woman her PI ID. "I'm investigating the murder of her friend Mya Berry. It's urgent I speak with her."

The receptionist's eyes widened and she stood. "One moment, please."

Indie waited next to Thomas until Hanna appeared, looking reluctant and apprehensive. Indie was good at reading people, as most detectives were, and this one had cornered cat written all over her. Seeing the negative energy radiating off the woman right now made Indie even more suspicious over why Hanna had avoided talking with her.

"Why did you want to speak to me?"

"I tried to contact you on numerous occasions," Indie said.

Hanna's eyes lowered briefly. "I already talked with the police a long time ago."

"The police haven't gotten very far," Indie informed her. "I was hired by Mya's family to investigate her murder. Is there somewhere we can go to talk?" She wasn't sure if the woman preferred privacy.

"Here is fine."

The waiting room was empty. Hanna took a chair and Indie sat next to her. Thomas took his post at the front window.

Hanna eyed him before focusing on Indie. "You never answered my question. Why do you want to talk to *me*?"

"Because I think you might be able to help me find your best friend's killer."

A troubled look came over Hanna. "I still can't believe she was murdered."

Was it denial that kept her from openly working with investigators? Indie highly doubted that.

"How could I possibly help with your investigation?" Hannah asked doubtfully.

"I'm thinking that perhaps there might be something the police missed, or maybe there's something you think is insignificant but could lead to a bigger clue," Indie explained.

"What do you want to know?"

"Walk me through the last few times you spoke with or saw Mya."

"We didn't see each other for weeks before her murder," Hanna said.

"Did you talk to her?" The police report said she hadn't. "On the phone? In person?"

"She called me about three days before she was killed."

Indie lifted a brow. Hanna must not remember lying to the authorities.

"You told the police you didn't talk to Mya for weeks," she said. Indie didn't take notes because she didn't want to make Hanna nervous—more nervous than she already was. She would summarize her visit when she returned home.

"Oh…" The woman seemed flustered. "I must have forgotten. We didn't talk long."

"What did you talk about?"

"Um…" Hanna averted her gaze before looking up at Thomas and then the receptionist. She turned back to Indie, who kept her expression blank.

"We just caught up on a few things. How are you doing, that sort of thing."

"And how *was* she doing?" Indie prodded.

"Fine. Working. Not much else."

"Did she mention Carl Brassard at all?" Indie asked.

"Carl?" Hanna's brow scrunched a little. "From high school?"

"Yes."

"No. Why?"

"They went out on a date shortly before her murder," Indie said. "He wanted to see her again but she wasn't interested."

Hanna looked genuine when she said, "I'm not surprised. Carl had a crush on her in high school, but she wasn't interested then. Frankly, I'm shocked she even went out on a date with him in the first place. She must have been bored."

Indie found it strange that Mya wouldn't tell her best friend about her date with a high school classmate. "Mya was the kind of woman who needed excitement?" she asked.

Hanna smiled. "Mya was active. She didn't like being stuck at home. She liked to go out and have fun."

"With you?" Indie murmured.

"No. I got married and our gallivanting days pretty much ended. We'd go to lunch and maybe a happy hour every once in a while, but over the last few years our friendship changed."

"Didn't Mya want to start a family? She dated a lot, it seems, after her marriage ended."

"I don't think she was ready to try marriage again," Hanna said. "She needed to be single for a while."

"What do you know about Carl?"

The woman shrugged. "He was sort of a wallflower in high school. Didn't have many friends. Wasn't popular. Some of the kids teased him. Why? Do you think he might have killed Mya?"

"Right now I don't know who killed her. I'm looking at everyone." Indie watched Hanna closely and noticed how she became apprehensive again.

She knew something.

"Hanna, what did you tell Mya the last time you spoke with her?"

"What?"

"You said it was a 'how are you doing' call. How were you doing?"

"Oh. F-fine. Same old thing. Married life and all," Hanna said nervously.

Indie decided to go on her hunch. "Did you and Mya have a falling out?"

The woman drew back her head and her face paled slightly, as though all the blood had left it. "N-no. We just grew apart. After her divorce."

Indie gave her a direct look, sober and suspicious. Hanna adjusted her body on the chair, crossing one leg over the other and clasping her hands on her lap.

"I've interviewed a lot of people," she said. "As a policewoman, as a detective, and now as a private investigator."

Hanna nodded her acknowledgment.

"There's something you aren't telling me."

Hanna lowered her head and after several seconds, met Indie's eyes. "It's true Mya and I drifted apart after her marriage."

"Okay. I believe you."

"But I don't know anything about her murder. I swear I don't."

"Okay, then what else drove you apart aside from Mya's marriage ending and her active lifestyle?"

"Nothing."

There was that nervousness again. The woman was a terrible liar.

"Hanna, you could help me solve her murder if you tell me everything you know leading up to the day she was killed. It's important not to leave out any detail."

"I can't help you." Hanna stood. "I've told you all I know."

Indie stood and handed her a card. "Please reconsider. I have reason to believe this could be the work of a serial killer. Regardless if it was someone she knew who murdered her, there is a dangerous man on the loose who's free to murder again."

Hanna took her card but said nothing.

Indie would be patient. She hoped the woman would come around after she thought about what Indie had said about a serial killer. If Mya meant anything to her, she would. Unless Hanna was the one responsible for her death, which Indie doubted based on the crime scene, and the signature left behind.

If Indie thought she'd get out of going on a date with him, she was wrong. He had reminded her this morning.

Wes was waiting for her when she arrived home from her day of investigating. He wondered how the case was going but refrained from asking just now. He had planned for them to go for a semi-casual dinner and some dancing afterward. She didn't strike him as the formal date type, and neither was he. The goal for tonight was to enjoy some downtime, and each other, of course, but not to wind up in bed together.

She looked him over, seeing he had dressed in jeans and a dress shirt. "I need a shower."

"No rush. We're going to The Country Ranch." They had live music that started at eight, leaving plenty of time for dinner first.

"That sounds appropriate," she said. And disappeared up the stairs.

Half an hour later, she emerged in jeans and a white blouse that revealed a hint of cleavage. She also had on a pair of cowgirl boots. A woman after his heart. She'd left her hair down, long silky strands draping over one shoulder. She had also applied a little makeup, her mascara making her stunning blue eyes stand out.

Thomas was driving them tonight. He had them at the restaurant in short order.

Wes put his hand on Indie's lower back as they entered The Country Ranch. With a high, darkly stained beam ceiling and romantic lighting, the open space sprawled to the kitchen in the back. A low wall divided the bar and band area.

The hostess brought them to their table, where they ordered wine and a lumpy-crab dip appetizer with spinach, mushrooms and grilled flatbread.

"Have you been here before?" Indie asked after he ordered without asking what she wanted.

"Yes. Trust me on the crab dip."

"I like crab."

"And I highly recommend their rib eye," he said.

"Did you and your wife come here?" she asked.

"Ex-wife," he corrected, seeing her eyes twinkle as she smiled and then took a sip of wine. "No. Charlotte didn't like it here. She was more of an Italian eater, which I'm not real big on."

"Me, either. Who doesn't like surf and turf?"

"I took a chance that you would like it here as much as I do," he said with a pleased grin.

"Who else did you take here?"

Clearly she was fishing for past girlfriend information. "I've never taken any dates here. I came here with friends and by myself after I was married."

"You have friends?" she asked in a teasing tone.

He chuckled. "My air force buddy comes out to see me sometimes. I don't keep in touch with anyone from high school. There's a family that owns a farm near my ranch. They invite me over for barbecues and holidays. They're sort of my adopted family. I've come here with Frank a time or two. Charlotte and I went to her family's home in Maine sometimes."

"Two friends. There's hope for you yet!"

He snorted. "Believe it or not, I have friends and many acquaintances through ranching. I just don't socialize much." That was probably why people had a misconception about him.

Their appetizer arrived and Wes ordered two rib eye plates, checking to see if Indie objected. She didn't. He liked her even more now. Damn.

"So why take me here?"

"I like it here. And I haven't been on a date in years."

She smiled before taking a bite of a chip, seeming pleased that he hadn't been on a date in a while. Neither had she, according to what he had learned so far about her.

"How did your meeting with that woman go today?" he asked.

Now she turned all business, taking a moment to swallow her chip. "She knows something. She and Mya talked just days before the murder. They talked about something Hanna didn't tell the police and refused to tell me. I hope I persuaded her to come and talk to me honestly."

"Hanna?"

"Mya's closest friend. I told her I thought we were dealing with a serial killer and any information she had could save a life. After I left her, I got to thinking why anyone would withhold information and the only thing that makes sense is if she knows someone who may have had a reason to kill Mya."

"You think she's protecting someone?"

"It's a theory. It's either that or she did it."

"What reason would she have for killing her best friend?" he asked.

"Maybe they had a falling out. Maybe Mya had an affair with her husband. Maybe it was money related. These are angles I plan to check out. I have a message in to Hanna's family, her mother and sister. The police interviewed a coworker Hanna was friendly with but not her family."

He met her eyes for a while, mesmerized by their sparkling beauty. A moment of warmth expanded in the space between them. He took in her face, smooth skin, full lips, sloping, proportioned nose. She had a slender neck and her breasts were just the right size. Not too big and not too small. But it was her mind that captivated him most. She had a dark past and there was much more to learn about her.

"I asked someone at DAI to start looking into similar cases in Texas and around the country," Indie said.

Wes suspected she'd stuck to the topic at hand to avoid acknowledging their chemistry. He didn't blame her for being careful. If she were the one divorced yesterday, he would be careful, too.

"That sounds time-consuming," he murmured.

"It could be," she said, sounding tense or maybe uncomfortable.

He sensed that her diffidence when it came to romance originated from more than his too-recent divorce. "Do you regret coming out on a date with me?" he asked quietly.

She took some time before answering. "If you ask my heart, I'd say no. If you ask my brain, I'd say yes."

"I suffer from the same dilemma," he admitted. This definitely was not a one-sided attraction. They felt the same about each other but the timing was wrong.

"Maybe the prudent thing for me to do is to go back home," she said. "I have bodyguards now."

She never really needed him in the first place. He hid the sting over her not being near him. "Is that what you plan to do?"

"That's the problem. I can't seem to plan anything when it comes to you." Her eyes roamed from his face down the front of him and back up again.

"Then maybe we just take this a day at a time," he said. Cautionary note: if she kept looking at him like that they wouldn't make it a day without cranking up the heat.

She nodded but didn't seem convinced. Clearly, her thoughts had taken the same path.

"I think we should just be friends until you're sure you're emotionally past your divorce," she said as though instilling a protective measure on their relationship.

He didn't tell her he was already emotionally past it. In fact, he should have gotten a divorce years ago. Funny, how Charlotte would end up being the one to have to work through her emotions. If anyone had told him that before Indie walked into his life, he would not have believed them.

He also didn't tell Indie that he wanted them to eventually become intimate. He didn't think he would be able to resist their chemistry any more than she would.

"Can I ask you something really personal?"

Indie met his eyes. "Sure." She sounded hesitant.

"What happened between you and that guy you were with after your divorce?" he asked.

"It didn't work out. Relationships end," she said.

That was a vague answer. Simplified. "Is he the one who disillusioned you?"

Indie lowered her head. Wes knew she did not like talking about this, but he needed her to open up to him if he was going to risk his heart again.

At last she raised her head, eyes full of remembered pain. "No. It was mostly Cole."

"Did he sleep with someone else?"

She shook her head. "Cole turned out to be different than I thought. He said he wanted a family but after we were married he said he changed his mind. Turns out he was a violent man. That's ultimately what ended us."

"You ended it with him?" That surprised him. She had seemed so torn over the breakup that he'd assumed the man had broken it off.

"Yes," she said. "It was me."

"How was he different?" Wes asked. He still had a feeling she wasn't telling him the whole story.

"I told you. I wanted a family and he wasn't going to give me one."

Wes caught the hint of defensiveness in her tone. She had ended it with Cole and given up trying to start a family of her own.

Having come from a similar background, he understood how it felt to discover the person you were with didn't want kids. But he still couldn't shake the feeling she withheld some information. Maybe she just didn't want to talk about it.

After dinner, the band began to play. Indie felt weighed down by all her thoughts and the things they'd talked about. Why had he asked her about Cole? She wished she could forget she'd ever met that man, or had anything to do with him. She wished she could forget him completely.

Wes stood and extended his hand.

A slow song had begun and other couples began to populate the dance floor. Indie took Wes's hand, feeling a dance was better than sitting here talking about her past.

He led her to the swaying couples and brought her close, not so close that they were meshed together, but close enough that he had one hand on her lower back. She put her hand on his shoulder, her other still cupped with his.

In the low light, his light blue eyes glowed in stark contrast to his dark hair. Once Indie met his gaze, she couldn't look away. The soft, live country music lulled her into the moment; so did their moving bodies and the warmth of his hands. He seemed to be trying hard to woo her with this date. Indie began to wonder why. He hadn't been driven to pursue her before. Why now? His ex-wife coming to see him? Her visits definitely had prompted a change in him, as though he was certain about the direction his life would take—without his ex-wife. That left him free to let this attraction they had for each other run its course.

But what did that mean for her?

Deciding not to dwell long on that, she let herself enjoy the music and dancing. When the beat picked up, she and Wes two-stepped.

"You dance well," he remarked as they went back to their table.

"I love country music. So did my parents. My dad taught me the two-step," she said, welcoming the fond memories. They were all she had now.

Wes smiled and Indie could tell that pleased him. He might be having optimistic thoughts about them now, but what about a few months from now? He could realize he had plenty of time to find the right woman, or maybe he would prefer to be single for a while. This night was enchanting but in the morning she would pour herself into work and keep her distance.

They danced until they were tired and then left. Indie hadn't smiled and laughed this much since she didn't even know when. Years perhaps.

Laughing as they left the building, she walked with Wes to his truck as he held her hand. All the way back to the ranch, she kept looking at him, making his mouth curve up in response to the happy curve of her own. A tiny voice tried to make her listen—telling her to be careful when she got back to the ranch—but she ignored it. Deliberately. She felt too darn good.

As they approached the house, Indie didn't want the night to end. Wes parked and they walked inside to a dark and quiet home. He switched on a light.

"Let's stay up and watch an old movie," he said.

"How old?" She laughed.

"Really old. *Casablanca*."

"Who doesn't like watching that every once in a while? Have to keep up on the classics." She was elated that they would spend a little more time together. Tomorrow would come soon enough.

Getting comfortable on the couch, she moved closer to Wes as he started the movie. He had an entire collection of old movies. She loved the hominess of it.

He put his arm behind her and she snuggled against him, resting her head in the crook of his arm as the show began. A few minutes into it she knew she wouldn't be able to stay awake. Her eyes drooped. One of her last thoughts was she had never felt safer or more content with a man.

Indie woke slowly the next morning. Feeling warm and lying against something that was a mixture of hard and soft. Seconds passed before she realized it was Wes's chest. Her eyes popped open and her heart skipped a beat. Her head was resting on his shoulder, her face so close to his that she could feel his even, slow breathing. While that captured her attention a moment, her leg draped over his dawned on her next. Their pelvises were touching. Her hand was on his ribs. His *bare* ribs. He must have unbuttoned his shirt before they had slipped into deep sleep. His arm curled around to her back.

Heart beginning to pound faster, she had to intake more air. Her fingers flexed into his smooth skin, and she slid her hand over more of his back, fascinated by the hard muscles beneath.

Wes's eyes opened.

She met them and waited for him to realize what she had.

He blinked a few times, waking further. Then she all but fell into the warmth that began to swirl between them.

"We must have fallen asleep during the movie," he said gruffly.

"How did we end up like this?" she asked, truly not knowing.

"I'm not sure. I think we fell asleep at the same time."

She vaguely remembered lying down. The ache in her right shoulder indicated she hadn't moved all night. Except maybe her leg…

She remained still and so did he. They just met each other's eyes. Indie could feel him immersed in the moment. His blue eyes darkened with growing desire. She wondered if hers looked the same way.

He slowly drew in for a kiss. The magic of last night must still have her under a spell. This morning she was supposed to go back to reality and thinking clearly, but the touch of his tongue to hers ignited her passion. As the caressing intensified, all thought of stopping fled.

She pushed his shirt off his shoulders. He took that as the go-ahead signal and began to undress her, unbuttoning her blouse. She leaned up a little to shrug it off. Then Wes brought her face back to his for another hungry kiss. She felt him unclasp her bra, and next, his warm hand on her breast.

Wes's back was against the sofa, so Indie stood and removed her bra and pants, seeing him take off his shirt and slide off his trousers. They worked in quick, jerky movements, as though they needed to hurry before either one changed their mind.

Indie had a chance to see Wes's bare body. He had magnificent proportion. He wasn't beefy but not slender, either. He had a beautiful physique.

She knelt on the couch and straddled him. It had been so long since she had been with a man like this that she wondered if the anticipation was hotter than it would be otherwise. Plus, she hadn't been with a man who looked as good naked as Wes did.

As Indie leaned forward, Wes glided his hands from her abdomen to her breasts. He ran his thumbs across her nipples. Indie lowered on top of him and planted a kiss on his mouth that heated rapidly to deeper joining.

Wes slid his hands to her rear as the kiss continued. Then he began pressing soft, sizzling kisses along her jaw and down her neck.

Indie propped herself up higher, allowing him access to her breasts. He took one into his mouth, his smoldering eyes meeting hers and driving her mad with desire. He treated both orbs and the tips of her sensitive nipples to his loving. Their breathing was the only sound in the room.

Wes moved back to her mouth and she gave him what she felt in another kiss. He groaned.

She lifted her head to look at him, awed over the sensation they created with each other.

"Are we sure about this?" he asked her breathlessly.

"No, but it feels too good to stop," she rasped back, kissing his mouth again.

"Yeah…it does." He put his big hand on the back of her head and held her for a commanding kiss. Then he pulled back to look up at her. "What about birth control?"

Did he seriously intend to ruin the moment? "I'm not…"

"I don't have condoms."

"I hate condoms," she said.

Breathing fast, flushed and all to ready to continue, she met his eyes and felt the silent communication. They both craved children.

All the uncertainties between them suddenly ceased to matter.

Indie lowered her mouth and pressed a soul-deep kiss to his lips. He answered in kind. She had never felt anything more powerful in her entire life.

No more words were necessary. He helped her position for his entry. She sank onto him, fireworks of hot sensation shooting through her body, tingling her limbs. She trembled with pleasure. Her breath came raggedly. She looked into his eyes as she began to grind on him, rocketing the sensations to unbearable heights.

He lifted his hips as she moved on him, creating a pounding that immediately sent her over the edge. Indie cried out. She was never vocal like this during sex. But Wes catapulted her out of herself into another realm. One that was full of love and thrilling emotion and physical ecstasy.

Indie curled up next to him and lay there catching her breath, feeling Wes's chest rise and fall as he did the same.

"How is this possible?" he murmured against her ear.

"I don't know," she said. Was it possible? Was this

just pure, carnal sex or was it the real thing? Indie only knew one thing. She had never felt like this before.

"So much for being friends first," she said, attempting to sound light, when inside she began to feel the gravity of the potential mistake they had both just made.

Chapter 10

Standing under the spray of water, Wes could not believe he had so recklessly dismissed the possibility Indie could become pregnant. That part of this morning kept repeating over and over in his mind. In the heat of passion, it hadn't mattered if they introduced a baby to their confusing relationship. He had allowed fantasy to take over. Or maybe *allowed* had nothing to do with it. Fantasy had taken over.

He didn't understand himself right now. So much in him had changed in such a short period of time. His entire outlook. He had gone from being devastated over his divorce to looking forward to embarking on a new life. Feeling happy. When was the last time he had felt happy?

A memory of his first wife rushed forth, front and

Treat Yourself with 2 Free Books!

**Claim up to FOUR NEW BOOKS & TWO MYSTERY GIFTS –
absolutely FREE!**

Dear Reader,

We both know life can be difficult at times. That's why it's important to treat yourself so you can relax and recharge once in a while.

And I'd like to help you do this by sending you this amazing offer of up to FOUR brand new full length FREE BOOKS that WE pay for.

This is everything I have ready to send to you right now:

Try **Harlequin® Romantic Suspense** books featuring heart-racing page-turners with unexpected plot twists and irresistible chemistry that will keep you guessing to the very end.

Try **Harlequin Intrigue® Larger-Print** books featuring action-packed stories that will keep you on the edge of your seat. Solve the crime and deliver justice at all costs.

Or **TRY BOTH!**

All we ask in return is that you answer 4 simple questions on the attached Treat Yourself survey. You'll get **Two Free Books** and **Two Mystery Gifts** from each series you try, *altogether worth over $20!* Who could pass up a deal like that?

Sincerely,

Pam Powers

Harlequin Reader Service

Treat Yourself to Free Books and Free Gifts.

Answer 4 fun questions and get rewarded.

▶ DETACH AND MAIL CARD TODAY! ▶

	YES	NO
1. I LOVE reading a good book.		
2. I indulge and "treat" myself often.		
3. I love getting FREE things.		
4. Reading is one of my favorite activities.		

TREAT YOURSELF • Pick your 2 Free Books...

Yes! Please send me my Free Books from each series I select and Free Mystery Gifts. I understand that I am under no obligation to buy anything, as explained on the back of this card.

Which do you prefer?

❑ **Harlequin® Romantic Suspense** 240/340 HDL GRCZ
❑ **Harlequin Intrigue® Larger-Print** 199/399 HDL GRCZ
❑ **Try Both** 240/340 & 199/399 HDL GRDD

FIRST NAME

LAST NAME

ADDRESS

APT.#

CITY

STATE/PROV.

ZIP/POSTAL CODE

EMAIL ❑ Please check this box if you would like to receive newsletters and promotional emails from Harlequin Enterprises ULC and its affiliates. You can unsubscribe anytime.

© 2022 HARLEQUIN ENTERPRISES ULC
™ and ® are trademarks owned by Harlequin Enterprises ULC. Printed in the U.S.A.

HI/HRS-520-TY22

center. They were cuddled together on an oversize recliner under a soft Afghan blanket. It was a week before Christmas.

"I have something to tell you," Rachel had said.

By the tone of her voice, he knew it was something important.

She had tipped her head up to look at him with happy eyes. "I'm a week late."

In that instant he knew she meant she might be pregnant. He had been so elated. His heart had soared with joy. And then she had been diagnosed with cancer. She'd lost the baby shortly after her first seizure.

But now, leaning his head back to let the water patter his skin, he could see so clearly that having a family had been the driving force of his relationship with Rachel. Like Indie, he had married with high hopes of a fairy-tale future. They both had lost all semblance of family at a young age.

Wes had idolized Rachel after her death. It hadn't been a true representation of what he had with her. It had been the beginning of the annihilation of his fanciful dreams, however.

Turning off the water, he dried off and got ready for the day. Then it was time to face Indie.

Out in the main living area, he saw her sitting at the table, laptop in front of her along with a steaming cup of coffee. She didn't look at him as he poured himself a cup.

"Hungry?" he asked.

"No. I'm fine."

She didn't look fine. Head low, she stared at the laptop screen but didn't work. She was tense.

"We need to talk," he said. He didn't want to talk, but it had to be done.

She finally lifted her head and looked at him. "I just slept with a man whose divorce isn't even forty-eight hours old."

"Yeah." Wes went to the table and sat across from her. "About that." He put his coffee cup down. "I agree it happened way too fast."

Indie turned her coffee cup in a circle on the table. Wes sensed she needed him to say more, but he didn't know what to say. He was as disconcerted as she was. What did she want him to say? She was disillusioned when it came to men. And didn't trust easily. He knew that much.

"I…" she began. "I can't…do that again."

He just looked at her because there was no way in hell he could promise her it wouldn't happen again. They couldn't stop themselves this morning. She herself initiated the sex. They both had ignored birth control. All for the gratification of desire. *Intense* desire.

In meeting his eyes, she understood what his silence meant.

"I should have never gone on that date with you," she said, sounding angry.

"So you do regret it."

"It was a stupid mistake. Just like this morning," she bit out.

Wes guessed she was angrier at herself than him.

"Well, that wasn't what I had planned. I just wanted us to get to know each other more," he said.

Her mood softened. "I know."

"What do you want to do?" he asked. He waited until he saw her register what he really asked.

"I should go home," she said.

"Will you?"

"Do you want me to?"

"No." He definitely did not want that. "I want you to stay."

Uncertainty crossed her face. She must have thought hard about going back home. Nothing was keeping her here now. Nothing, other than him.

"What do you suggest we do, then?" she asked.

"Let it run its course. I'll try to keep my hands off you and you'll try to keep your hands off me. Beyond that, we'll have to see."

She looked down with a sigh, and then finally lifted her head again to meet his eyes. "I should go home."

"Why? Are you afraid of being disappointed again?" he asked. "Don't say anything about my divorce. My marriage was over years ago. It's all right if you don't trust me yet, but stop projecting the future. Stay right here, right now. With me."

Her face took on an anguished look. "Why?"

"I like you, and I think you like me, too."

"It's just sex, Wes. I need more than that."

"Right now you do?" he asked, already knowing the answer.

She put her head on her hands, elbows on the table.

"No." Then she raised her head to look at him again. "But I don't want sex, either."

He grinned and then chuckled a little. She sure was adorable when she was confused over her own feelings.

"This isn't funny," she said.

"It could be."

She eyed him as though he had lost his mind.

"I refrain, you refrain. That's the deal," he said.

"That's the deal." She nodded but didn't seem convinced. "I'm going to talk to Carl Brassard today. I'll have my bodyguards."

Apparently they were finished talking. "Okay. I'll be where I always am. Working on the ranch."

Then he headed for the door, trying to suppress another chuckle. "Good luck today," he called over his shoulder. "See you tonight."

She knew she was being irrational. Indie walked toward the auto parts store where Carl worked. She should absolutely go back home and never see Wes again. Why was walking away so difficult?

Because Wes intrigued her.

Because she had never met a man who interested her this much, who matched her on so many levels, sex being just one of them.

Because, for the life of her, she could not turn her back on the possibility—one last chance—of finding that ever-elusive true love.

It didn't matter that she was scared out of her mind. What if this didn't turn out to be true love? It wasn't love. Not at all. She didn't know him well enough. Or was she wrong—could it be, after all, that this was the budding of true love? She was too afraid to hope. So she'd do as Wes said—stay right here, right now. And right now, she had a person of interest to question. She welcomed the distraction.

Inside the well-lit store, with her bodyguards in tow, she saw an older man behind the counter ringing up a customer's purchases. Indie didn't see anyone else. She waited for the customer to finish. Her bodyguards hung back, knowing to keep a little distance.

"Hello," she said to the man. "Indie Deboe, PI." She showed him her DAI identification. "Is Carl Brassard here?"

The man's face glowered. "What'd he do now?"

"I'm only here to ask him a few questions about a girl he knew from high school. He isn't in any trouble." Yet.

"Carl," the man yelled over his shoulder.

A few seconds later, Carl appeared, blond hair cut in a neat, short style.

"There's a detective here to talk to you," the man said. Presumably, this was Carl's father.

Carl took note of the older man's displeasure and then faced Indie with a confused look.

"Hi, Carl. I'm Indie Deboe. I'd like to talk to you about Mya Berry."

He immediately grew wary. "Me? Why me?"

"I know you went out on a date with her and went to see her at her place of employment. Can you tell me why you did that?"

"She wasn't answering my calls and I wanted to find out why and also if she would like to keep seeing me."

"And when she said she wasn't interested, how did you react?"

"I wasn't happy but if she doesn't like me she doesn't like me."

Indie took out her notepad and pen. "There was a restraining order against you two years ago for stalking. Is it fair to say you began stalking Mya?"

Carl shook his head adamantly. "No. That restraining order was bull. Just because I need the women I see to communicate their feelings to me doesn't make me a dangerous man. I don't like it when women just blow me off. It's rude."

"So you need them to explain why they don't want to see you again?" Indie asked as neutrally as she could. But it seemed odd that anyone would expect someone they barely knew to offer any explanation. Why did it matter? If a woman wasn't answering a man's calls it meant she didn't want to talk to him. Done deal.

"Yes."

"Do you tell them that?"

"I left Mya a message. Several, in fact, saying I only needed to talk to her."

"You were also arrested for assault," Indie said.

Carl's expression grew annoyed. "I'm straightening out my life, even though my dad doesn't believe me yet." He glanced back at the man, who hovered close, either pretending to organize a shelf or actually doing so.

"Would you have assaulted Mya if she continued to ignore your requests to talk?" Indie asked.

"No. That assault happened when I was much younger and couldn't handle rejection well. I've changed since then."

She debated the truth of that. "How did you feel when Mya told you to leave her place of work and that she didn't want to see you again?"

"Disappointed. I liked her in school. I thought it would have been great if we could at least hang out together for a while to see if there was any connection. She apparently knew there wasn't after *one date*."

The way he said "one date" clued Indie into how offended he was. "When was the last time you saw her?"

"That day I went to her work," he said. "She made it abundantly clear she wanted nothing to do with me."

"When did you learn she was killed?"

"I heard about it on the news." He seemed to fall into a regretful pondering. "It was shocking."

"Where were you the night she was murdered?"

"I closed here. Left around eight and stopped at a pub for a few beers. I think I got home around eleven."

Indie glanced at his father, who nodded his head. "It was about that time when I heard him come home."

"You live with your parents?" Indie asked.

"Yes." He took out his phone and navigated a bit.

"This is my bank account. I used my debit card to pay my tab that night." After a while longer, he showed Indie a page of his account. The line item was the same date as the night Mya had been killed.

Mya's time of death was estimated to be between 3:00 and 5:00 a.m. and she left the bar, where she had gone with her friends, at 11:00 p.m. Carl had probably arrived home when Mya left the bar. It would have taken her about fifteen minutes to get home, and she'd disappeared before getting into her house. Carl's house was a considerable distance away. He couldn't have made it to Mya's house before she got home and into her house. All Indie had to do was confirm the time he left the pub.

With a sick feeling in her stomach, she thanked Carl and left. This was looking more and more like a serial killer case.

Walking with big bodyguard Thomas to her left and tall bodyguard Samuel to her right, Indie spotted a familiar car parked in the lot of the auto parts store, a black Charger. The man wore sunglasses and a baseball hat, but she saw his dark hair.

"That's him." She pointed to the car. She watched the stranger purse his mouth in irritation, obviously displeased she was accompanied by two formidable men.

Thomas and Samuel retrieved their guns.

The stranger reversed with tires squealing, and raced out of the lot.

Indie's heart pounded frantically. Her face felt cold and numb. That sick feeling intensified.

Inside the car, Samuel and Thomas kept searching for the Charger. Indie did, too. How had the stranger found her? If he selected his victims carefully, he would study them first. Had he seen Mya go on her date with Carl? Had he seen Carl visit her at work? Everything in her resonated that he must have. He must have known a lot about Mya before he captured and killed her.

About a week ago, Indie had found a lovely mare on the ranch that she'd begun to visit every day. She was a palomino with a beautiful gold coat and white mane. But it was her eyes Indie loved the most. Brown windows into a gentle but playful soul, they spoke to Indie. She found out from Phil that her name was Honey—not very original, but it suited her. Indie felt a connection to her the moment they met.

She had taken to walking every morning for exercise. The ranch had many dirt roads that served as access routes to the various pastures. On the first day she started that routine, she spotted Honey in the pasture. With a cowgirl hat shading her from the bright sun in a clear blue sky, Indie had stood in awe of how pretty the animal was. The mare had lifted her head and watched her a while, and then, curiosity getting the best of her, had walked to the fence.

Honey had checked her out, wary at first, but after a bit of silent communication, she'd stepped close enough for Indie to touch her. Indie had avoided her face at first, petting her neck and just telling her what a sight she was.

Today was a lot like that day: warm and bright, with no clouds. Honey saw her and, with no hesitation, walked toward her. As Indie had begun to do, she climbed over the fence and went to the horse.

"Good morning," she said.

The horse nickered and bumped her head against her.

Indie smiled, the affection always making her feel so peaceful and full of delight. "I'm going to have to see if I can ride you some day."

As on all the other days, Indie saw no other palominos in the pasture.

"You're one of a kind," Indie said.

"Kind of like you."

Indie turned to see Wes atop a chestnut gelding, devastatingly handsome in wranglers and a cowboy hat. She hadn't seen much of him since their lusty morning tryst. She'd made it her goal to avoid him for a while, but still couldn't bring herself to leave. Now she had more of a reason to stay. She was beginning to really love this ranch.

"I see you've met Honey," he said.

"Yes." Indie turned to look up at the mare's golden brown eyes and blond lashes fanning out from the upper lids. The horse lifted her lip and nipped at her face, making Indie laugh softly.

"She doesn't take to just anyone," Wes said. "She's high-spirited and quite independent."

"Really." Indie looked at Honey again. She didn't strike her as high-spirited, but she had yet to ride the mare.

Like a moth to light, she walked to the fence. Honey followed.

"We became friends when I started walking every day." Her hat shaded her eyes from the glaring sun and she could see how Wes looked at her, eyes a darker blue under the brim of his hat and rather smoldering with masculine interest.

"Are those new jeans?" he asked.

She glanced down at her wranglers, feeling a flash of self-consciousness. She had been struck with an impulse to dress like she belonged on a ranch. The attire felt natural but she also felt like she was getting too accustomed to life here. Imposing, maybe.

"Yes."

"Hat, too."

"Guilty." She raised her palm.

"You're beautiful like that," he said.

Not knowing what to say, she said nothing and just fought a rising flush.

"I mean…you're beautiful anyway but…the look is perfect on you."

Okay, he could stop anytime now.

At that moment, Honey decided to put her head over Indie's shoulder, breaking the awkwardness. Curving her arm under the mare's head, Indie rubbed her cheek and leaned into the hug.

"Wow," Wes said as he observed them. "You really do have a way with horses."

"Yeah. Who would've thought?" She laughed as Honey ran her head along Indie's shoulder. She turned to plant a kiss on her soft muzzle.

"I didn't see any others like her," Indie said.

"I still have a couple of others. They are in another pasture because Honey gets a little rough on them."

"Her?" Indie eyed the horse, who was the sweetest thing in her opinion.

"She's not very friendly with other horses. She likes to be in charge." He gestured to the other horses in this pasture. "None of these horses care about her attitude."

"So you're a feisty one, huh?" Indie said to the horse.

"My grandfather bred palominos on the ranch he owned. Honey is from that line. She's actually Honey the fourth, descended from a champion show horse."

"Well, no wonder she cops an attitude."

She looked up at him and fell into the way his eyes regarded her, and felt heat singing through her from the heady male interest glimmering in their mesmerizing blue depths.

"How's the case coming along?" he asked.

"It's not. Hanna still won't talk. Even though I know she knows something. Carl is ruled out. I have calls in to other counties but I haven't heard back. If the killer has killed before, I'm beginning to think he did so in another state. I've got someone at DAI looking into that." They fell into another moment of silent staring. "How's ranching going?" She didn't tell him about the dark-haired stranger she had seen. He was already protective of her and she needed to stay zeroed in on her job.

"Same old. I sold a few horses a few days ago

at auction. Signed up a couple more customers for breeding. All in all, it's been a lucrative, busy week."

"That's good." It was Friday and they faced a weekend of living in the same house. "Well, I should head back and see if I have any messages." She faced Honey and kissed her again. "You behave." Then she went to the fence and climbed over.

"I'll give you a lift," Wes said.

Indie looked down the long dirt road and up at the sky. It was shaping up to be a hot afternoon. "Okay."

He gave her the use of his stirrup. She stuck her foot in and grabbed onto his sturdy arm to swing herself up behind him. What had seemed like a harmless offer now felt way too intimate. She had nothing to hold onto except him. Her hand rested against his six-pack stomach.

"Where are Thomas and Samuel?" Wes asked.

"I told them to take the weekend off." She also didn't let them come on her walks. She needed some time to herself.

"Is that safe?"

"No one knows where I am. Except Julien, but he won't tell anyone," she said. Besides, she was tired of having them follow her around all the time. She felt safe here on the ranch. Leaving was another story, but she had no plans to do that this weekend.

"I can arrange to saddle up Honey tomorrow and we can ride down to the stream for lunch if you want. I know a great spot."

She pursed her lips. "Are you asking me out on another date?"

"No. Just something I like to do to enjoy the ranch."

She could appreciate that. And she found herself looking forward to being in a place he obviously loved, a favorite spot on his beloved ranch. A ranch that was claiming a piece of her heart as well.

Indie took in the smooth movement of the horse and the way it made her rock and occasionally caused a gentle bump against Wes.

She was glad when they made it back to the stable. Dismounting, she said, "Thanks."

"See you later."

Indie walked back to the house and entered her office. Funny, how she now thought of it as her own office. She had added touches, like a plant, and had rearranged some things. Wes didn't mind. He told her to make it hers. Of course he did because Indie had a feeling he wanted her here permanently. Sometimes, though, she sensed his hesitation. She didn't know if he was wary of her or if he had second thoughts every once in a while.

Picking up her phone, she saw she had a message. She listened to it.

"Ms. Deboe, this is Hanna Foster. I need to talk to you. Please call me as soon as you can."

Indie's heart pumped with excitement. She pressed the phone number Hanna had left.

The woman answered on the second ring.

"There's something I need to tell you," Hanna said without preamble.

"Let's meet somewhere," Indie suggested.

"There's a coffee shop in town. The Great Bean."

Indie knew the place. "It'll take me about twenty minutes to get there."

"Okay. I'll see you soon."

After hanging up, Indie had a feeling of foreboding. Hanna had sounded desperate to meet and talk. And had seemed downright scared. While Indie always made sure she met with witnesses, suspects and people of interest in person, she had never had a case like this—one so dangerous.

Indie tried to call Thomas and Samuel but neither answered. They had the weekend off. She gathered her things, making sure she had extra rounds of ammo and a spare gun in her boot. The she headed for the door, thinking she'd like to have Wes with her as much for security as for his company. That horseback ride had done something to her for sure.

Outside, she saw him walking toward the house. It was around five, close to dinnertime. He stopped before her.

"Going somewhere?" he asked, his eyes taking in her form the way they had when he'd come upon her with Honey.

"Hanna called. She wants to talk."

"Want some company?"

She smiled. "Yes." That was exactly what she wanted, too much.

Wes thought he might be making a mistake, inviting Indie to get close to him again. Inviting himself, too. At The Great Bean, he opened the door for her and they stepped inside, scanning the crowd for anyone suspicious. He stayed close to Indie, ready to get her out of harm's way in an instant.

A blonde woman sat alone at a four-seat booth. Wes followed Indie there. The blonde looked nervous. He was no professional at reading people but this one made it obvious.

"Thank you for agreeing to meet." Indie sat on the bench and made room for Wes. "I hope you don't mind that I brought a bodyguard. This case is dangerous."

Hanna looked concerned. "Is the killer after you?"

"Yes, but let's not get into that. I really appreciate you talking to me again. What can you tell me, Hanna?"

The woman lowered her head and gripped her water glass a little hard. "This isn't easy for me to do."

"Take your time." Indie waited several seconds. "Why is it hard for you?"

After a few more seconds, Hanna lifted her head. "Because it involves my husband."

Oh boy. This could be a big break. "What's your husband's name?" Indie asked softly.

"Eddie."

"Mya must have known him pretty well, given the two of you were friends."

Hanna nodded a few times, slowly.

"Did they have an affair?" Indie asked.

Wes wondered why she had asked and presumed it was her natural investigative instinct.

Hanna wiped a spring of tears from her eyes. "Yes.

I followed him one day after he got off work. He told me he was working late, but he didn't. He drove to Mya's house. I confronted him when he got home. He said he didn't love her and that it was just sexual. I was crushed. I couldn't believe he would do something like that. I always trusted him. It's like I don't really know him as well as I thought."

"Did you tell the police he was having an affair?" Indie knew she hadn't. There was nothing about it in the files.

"No. I was too humiliated. Mya was murdered just a few days after I found out."

"So your conversation with her three days prior to her murder wasn't a 'catch up' call," Indie said.

Hanna again lowered her head and then raised it to meet Indie's eyes. "No. She called to apologize. I was upset and didn't accept it. She said she didn't intend on getting involved with my husband. It just happened. She used the same excuse that Eddie did. Told me it wasn't love, it was just sex. And that she wasn't interested in a serious relationship." She blew out a breath. "I asked her why it had to be my husband. If all she needed was sex, why couldn't she have chosen someone else? She said she wished it had been someone else. She never meant to hurt me." Hanna shook her head slowly. "I don't understand how anyone could do that. She had a choice. She could have chosen to resist her urges. I think she always wanted my husband. She was envious of what we had and bitter over what she didn't have in her own marriage."

Hanna fell silent in her thoughts. Wes saw how

Indie allowed her time. Like him, she saw how upset she was and hoped she would keep talking.

Indie glanced at Wes, who sat quietly beside her, keeping an eye out for suspicious activity through the window while he observed and listened to her interaction with Hanna.

"I have so many mixed feelings," Hanna said. "I'm angry with her. I'm horrified by the way she died. I miss her. Sometimes I'm glad she's dead for what she did to me and then I feel terrible for having those thoughts."

"What about your husband? How do you feel about him?" Indie asked.

Wes suspected more than humiliation kept Hanna from telling the police about his affair.

"He wants to make our marriage work," she said. "He still loves me. He thinks he had the affair because we sort of got into a rut after our kids were born. It's like we never fully adjusted to the new way of life." She sighed. "I have to agree, but he shouldn't have slept with anyone. I wish I didn't love him. I should kick him right out of my life. But I can't." Hanna looked anguished. After a few moments, she said, "Eddie wasn't home the night Mya went missing."

Wes's attention spiked.

"Where was he?" Indie asked the question he wanted to.

"He said he was out with friends, but I went to the pub where he said he was going and he wasn't there. I drove by Mya's place and saw his car there, parked in the street. He was inside. Waiting for her."

"What time was that?"

"Around eight."

Mya got off work at eleven. Wes didn't think Eddie would have waited three hours for her. But he might have gone back.

"What time did he get home?" Indie asked.

"A little after ten."

"Was he home the rest of the night?"

"Yes." Hanna wore a worried look. She was at odds with her husband but still loved him and feared he might be a suspect in a murder investigation.

"Mya was at work until eleven that night," Indie said. "And I don't see a motive for Eddie to murder her. You knew about the affair. Why would he kill her after that came to light?" And from the way Hanna had described it, Eddie seemed like he had good intentions for his marriage, other than sleeping with his wife's best friend.

"What's Eddie like?" Indie asked just in case. "Is he violent? Controlling?"

Hanna shook her head. "No. He is calm and friendly. He treats me well. That's why it's such a shock he did what he did."

Indie glanced at Wes again. He caught her look, having been listening most of the time but acutely aware of their surroundings.

"Mya was a beautiful woman," she said to Hanna. "And you yourself said she liked to be active, social. Maybe a little wild?"

The woman nodded, looking like she felt better now that she'd confessed the truth.

"Thank you for coming forward, Hanna," Indie said. "You've been a big help."

"I'm sorry for lying before," she said.

"You made it right today." Wes stood and Indie scooted out of the booth. "I hope everything works out between you and your husband."

Hanna's eyes fell, giving away her doubt. As they left the coffee shop, Wes didn't think she'd be able to stay with a man who slept with another woman, no matter how much she loved him. The trust would be gone. Plus, if a man truly loved his wife, he would never hurt her by making such a huge mistake.

Thinking back on her own mistakes and heartaches, Indie mused that she'd learned that lesson the hard way. Wes had, too, she supposed. Charlotte had cheated on him. How did he feel about that, really? When his wife left him he would have taken her back. Now that he had met Indie, his view had changed.

Spotting a dark-haired man walking down the sidewalk, her senses came alive. Wes noticed as well, and put his body between the man and her. The man had been looking at them, at her as he approached. He was about the same build as her abductor. They reached Wes's truck as the man drew nearer. She could see him clearly now.

"It's not him." Indie breathed several times, her adrenaline in high gear. Relief flooded her in a wave.

Wes opened the truck door for her. She got in and leaned her head back against the seat, heart gradually slowing. He started driving and she reverted back to the thoughts she'd been having as she left the coffee shop.

"This might sound like a silly question," she said. "But how did you feel when you found out your wife slept with someone else?"

His head turned as though he was taken aback by the question. At last he said, "Not good."

She breathed a brief laugh at his sarcasm. "Well, yes, that's a given, but how did you really feel?"

He didn't answer right away. "Betrayed, mostly. Angry. And I guess in some ways, not surprised. I didn't admit to the not surprised part until much later."

"Because you believed you loved her."

"And I believed she loved me. She told me sleeping with that man didn't mean anything. That she wanted me. You see, that's what Charlotte does. She starts to follow what's really in her heart and then she goes back to where she feels safe. She couldn't handle change."

All of that he had realized after meeting Indie. She didn't know quite how to deal with that, or, more importantly, what it meant for her down the road. She had a fleeting thought to just go with it and stop trying to protect herself from the future, but she had made too many mistakes with men to be impulsive right now.

"Why do you ask?" Wes asked.

"It didn't seem like you cared very much. You wanted her back."

"What bothered me the most was her betrayal. It

doesn't matter she didn't love me and I didn't love her. It becomes a matter of integrity. A person who can betray their spouse's trust is someone who doesn't care enough about others. Who wants to be with someone like that?"

Indie turned her head toward the window, even more apprehensive about getting involved with him. She'd had an affair while she was married. Even though her marriage was destructive and abusive, she had still lied and been unfaithful. Her husband had deserved it but she almost hadn't survived the repercussions. She sucked in a ragged breath. Would Wes, who had been the victim of someone cheating and lying, see it as justified or put her in the category of someone not to be trusted?

Chapter 11

Dai sent over some cases that could be similar to Mya's murder. All of them were women. Indie sat on the sofa in the office, Wes beside her. On the coffee table they had piled up printed copies of the files. He had taken a bigger interest in the investigation since talking with Hanna. Indie wasn't sure if it was an excuse to be near her or if the dramatic change in the investigation compelled him. A serial killer on the loose terrified and horrified her as much as what made him that way fascinated her. As a normal person with empathy, she could never understand what drove a person to kill methodically.

Indie liked being with Wes, so she didn't protest when he said he wanted to help. Even while her defenses warned of the danger to her heart, she welcomed his company. He was such a good person. Kind. Strong. Not conceited at all. Real. Yes, Wes was a *real* man.

"This one was found in some trees along a two-lane highway in Wyoming," he said, breaking into her thoughts and returning her to the task at hand. "Megan Walker was raped and stabbed fifteen times. Happened six years ago. She was taken right from her home."

The similarities might link the crime to Mya's. "Was there signs of a break-in or a struggle?"

Wes searched through the report. "No break-in, but there were signs of a struggle."

"He must have known her." Indie jotted down that important clue. If the killer knew Megan, he may not be a serial killer.

"The detectives who worked her case didn't find a suspect who knew her," Wes said.

"He could have deliberately met her, gotten to know her enough so he wouldn't be a stranger. Megan probably hadn't told anyone about him. I didn't find anything in the report indicating there had been a new acquaintance in her life." Indie wondered if he did that with all the women. She doubted it since Mya had been abducted in front of her house and no one who knew her was a suspect. Just like all the other cases. "Was she positioned?" she asked.

"The report doesn't mention anything about that."

"I found one from California, but the woman was shot after being raped. No blindfold," Indie said.

They continued to read through the documents.

Every once in a while Indie glanced over at Wes, his handsome profile drawing her in. It hadn't escaped her notice that they both had taken an interest in each other's livelihood. She loved his ranch and all the animals and he clearly was sucked into her investigation.

She came across another case in Wyoming. "Where did that other Wyoming murder take place?" she asked.

Wes picked up the pages on the Megan Walker case. "She was from Laramie and was found in the Medicine Bow National Forest."

"A woman named Tessa Chase was from Saratoga and her body was found off Highway 130. Raped and stabbed…and a piece of a torn scarf was found near her body, caught on a branch." She looked up and met his eyes.

"Geez. That is so horrible and morbid," he said.

"They all are." She read more on the Tessa Chase case. "Where is the rest of the scarf? Did he take it with him? Like a souvenir? Maybe the killer had her blindfolded while he raped her, and took a perverse liking to her scarf." The scarf likely belonged to Tessa and could have ended up torn as she fought for her life. Did he get his jollies in the sounds the women made but didn't like seeing their eyes? All speculation at this point but things Indie would need to investigate.

"Takes a sturdy heart to do this kind of thing," Wes said gruffly.

"I work for the victims. It took me a while to get used to this, to be able to stomach it. It still gets to me, but as long as I stay focused on the investigation I do all right. And I never lose sight of my purpose. These killers have to be caught before they hurt anyone else."

Wes continued to look at her. Tingles spread through her and she warmed.

"I don't mean to compare, or keep bringing her up, but Charlotte didn't do anything with her life. She didn't work. She liked shopping and going out to lunch." His gaze held a sea of admiration and, more, attraction. "I was so busy with the ranch that it didn't matter then, but it does now."

She smiled softly, allowing herself to absorb the compliment. "Get back to work," she teased.

He chuckled and returned to the documents.

She glanced over and caught another look from him. Indie smiled and he smiled back. She felt like a girl again, flirting with a new love interest. It reminded her of how she'd felt when she first met her ex-husband. She had been so full of hope. When the signs pointed toward the possibility of something good and lasting with him, she had felt giddy with excitement and happiness. But her feelings now were more intense than back then.

Wes looked at her once more and must have seen her sobering. He began concentrating on the documents. She finally did the same. They studied in companionable silence.

So far, most of the victims in the reports DAI sent her had been stabbed. Some weren't raped and some were killed in their homes. She didn't find any evidence the bodies had been moved, and other than the one crime with the scarf, none were blindfolded.

"Anything else?" she asked Wes.

"I don't think so. One went missing after going to a bar and was found raped and murdered about two miles away in a park."

That sounded like it had potential. "What did the crime scene look like?"

"She was stabbed twice and found partially clothed. Lower half bare."

Wes probably thought this wasn't a match because the victim had only been stabbed twice. Indie leaned over to view the page he held. "Was she moved?"

"I don't know. No blindfold. Her car was still in the bar parking lot, so she must have been abducted there, or gone willingly."

Indie leaned closer and began reading. Cheryl Sanchez was twenty-two and from Park City, Utah. The first thing Indie noticed from the crime scene photos was that her jeans were draped over her face. Her arms were above her head and her legs were straight and spread. Indie saw nothing in the report to indicate the detectives had found evidence of the body being moved. Which meant she had been killed there. The area surrounding the victim was wooded. There was some ground vegetation but the body lay on dirt and pine needles.

She picked up the photo and held it closer to her face, searching for clues. Finally, she saw what appeared to be a scuff in the dirt between the woman's feet, as though her heel had been dragged. The mark must have been left after death. Any victim wouldn't keep her legs apart after her assailant got off her. She would try to get away. Indie imagined the poor woman fighting for her life. Had she struggled when the killer had finished raping her?

Indie saw brush marks in the dirt. Pine needles were more numerous away from the body and almost clean near it, as though someone had erased footprints. She checked the notes and found the detectives had noted the same. So there must have been a struggle, and then, after the killer stabbed her, he probably positioned her body.

She found a picture of the woman's face without the jeans covering it. Indie couldn't tell if something had been used to blindfold her, but the report contained evidence of fibers that weren't from the denim. Would they match the torn piece of scarf from Tessa's crime scene?

Indie searched the photos until she found one of the torn piece of scarf. The pattern was identical to the one at Mya's crime scene.

A feeling came over her, something dark but telling. "This is our killer." She needed DNA and trace evidence testing done. "This matches the blindfold on Mya's body."

"Holy hell," he said.

Megan's murder was the earliest of the four. Had the killer begun covering his victim's eyes after this murder? What about the first victim had bothered him—if she was the first victim, and if these women were all killed by the same man?

Her cell phone rang. She didn't recognize the number but answered anyway. "Indie Deboe, PI."

"Ms. Deboe," a man said. "This is Detective Joyce over in Tucson, Arizona. I got a call from someone at Dark Alley Investigations, who told me about a case you're working."

Indie's pulse picked up with a surge of anticipation. She put her phone on the table and pressed the speaker so Wes could hear.

"The Mya Berry case?" she asked.

"Yes. I wanted to talk to you personally rather than work through your agency."

"Of course. I want the same."

"I've got two cases here that I've long suspected are the work of a serial killer," Detective Joyce told her. "The crime scenes match yours almost exactly. The victims were raped and stabbed multiple times and the bodies moved and positioned."

"You're sure they were positioned?"

"Yes. One was propped up against a tree with her legs apart and the second was placed on a picnic table in similar fashion. The picnic table suggests he's progressively getting bolder with the staging. The table was in a dark area of a park, but the location of the crime was about twenty feet from there, just off a hiking and biking trail. And now I see he's placed a body in a cemetery."

She didn't have to ask how he had known where the murder occurred. There would have been blood and possibly other signs of a struggle.

"Was there a blindfold?" she asked.

"No, but pants were dropped over the first victim's face and a light hoodie over the other."

Chills raced down Indie's arms. She met Wes's equally stunned face.

"When did your murders occur?" Indie queried.

"First victim was two years ago. Her name is Katrina Daniels. Second one, Briana Gray, was six months after that."

"Mya was murdered almost a year ago," Indie said. "And just tonight we found three other murders that could be the signature of this serial killer. First one was six years ago, second two years after that and the third one year following. In the third, jeans were covering her face and fibers not matching the denim were discovered. In the second case, a piece of torn scarf was discovered."

"There were fibers in my second victim's crime scene but not the first." He paused as all three of them registered the magnitude of this finding. If the fibers matched the torn piece, that meant the killer had used the same scarf in all of the murders. He blindfolded them and then took the scarf with him, using clothing at the crime scene to cover their faces.

"In the Tessa Chase case, the second murder, the pattern of the torn scarf matches the blindfold in Mya's case," Indie said. "In the first murder there was no blindfold, but a shirt was draped over the victim's face. No sign of positioning and no foreign fibers."

No fibers because the killer didn't obtain the scarf until he murdered Tessa. He had found a coveted souvenir, one he must have relished using on subsequent victims.

"He left the scarf but that doesn't mean he's finished killing," Detective Joyce stated.

"I agree. I'm going to see if I can find out if Mya was wearing something like a scarf the day she was killed, something that wasn't recovered at the crime scene."

"Like a new scarf for the killer?" Wes asked.

Indie looked at him. "Exactly."

"I'd like to work with you on this," Detective Joyce said. "I suspect there are more victims than these. The killer could have murdered women every six months or so."

That was entirely possible. Indie and Wes hadn't found Detective Joyce's two murder cases, but they hadn't finished going through all the records yet. But they could establish a timeline, at least the beginnings of one. The first two murders had occurred in Wyoming. The third in Utah, and now two more in Tucson. Had the killer traveled through Las Vegas and after leaving Tucson, gone to Texas? One thing was clear. The killer was mobile. And yes, Indie agreed 100 percent there had to be more.

She had to stop him before he struck again.

One thing bothered her, though. If the serial killer was getting bolder, why had he gone after Indie? Had he been more confident with the police doing the investigation? DAI had a worldwide reputation. All the killer would have to do was conduct a little research online to learn what he was up against.

Leaving the scarf he had used in multiple murders was another bold move. Surely he had to know the police would connect it to previous murders. Her best guess was that he wanted them to know the killings were done by the same man. He was proud of what he had done. As sickening as that was, it fit the profile of a serial killer. He thought he was smarter than the detectives working the cases. Well, he wasn't smarter than her. Indie was going to catch him.

The next morning over breakfast, Wes had told Indie he was going to breed some horses and, as he expected, she lit up with enthusiasm. He kept his soaring satisfaction to himself and told her to meet him in the breeding shed at one.

Now, inside the breeding shed, he kept watch on the open double barn doors, wishing he wasn't so distracted. Breeding was his bread and butter. So much went into this operation, from the health of his horses to the safety of his crew. Stallions could get wild with the zest to get to a mare.

His breeding shed was a good size. He stood with his arm on the padded half wall in front of the empty stall.

He saw Indie enter the breeding shed, beautiful and radiant and full of interest in the animals.

Charlotte had been in this barn once during breeding and she had rushed out and vomited after seeing a stallion penetrate a mare. He was apprehensive over how Indie would react. To him, breeding was an art and he valued his horses' participation in the operation.

"Did I miss it?" Indie asked.

"Oh, no. The teaser just left."

"Teaser?"

He smiled. "We use another stallion to prepare a mare for being mounted by her intended."

"Her *intended*?" She breathed a laugh. "Sounds like a real courtship."

"It is, in a way." Breeding horses was a strategic process. He looked around the breeding shed designed to protect the horses in case things got out of control. "I'll give you a tour. It'll be a few minutes before they're ready."

He led her to the anteroom, where a big, chestnut stallion was being readied. "He's already been washed." Wes pointed to the halter. "We use a different halter when we take a stallion to the breeding shed. It's one of the ways we let the animal know he's on his way here, and what awaits him."

The stallion pranced sideways and snorted, excited to get moving.

"The mares are led in through another entrance," Wes said, walking from the anteroom back into the main area of the breeding shed. As though on cue, a mare stepped through a wide and tall doorway.

The breeding manager led her across nonslip floors that were installed as a safety measure for both animal and human. He noticed how Indie tested the grip with her booted feet and fell in love with her a little more.

The mare, which was named Moxy, trotted with her handler toward the area where the breeding would take place. When the handler had her settled, the stallion was brought in. He strained against the halter, his eyes trained on the mare. She was positioned before a padded half wall. The handler went to stand behind it as the stallion neared.

Another handler put on a thick, leather neck shield—something for the stallion to bite when mounting, a method of balance. Wes glanced at Indie and reveled in her rapt expression. People had varying reactions to seeing horses mate like this. Wes kept it as close to the natural way as possible, but he had a business to run. Chosen stallions were paired with chosen broodmares. But nature always took its course. A mare was ready and a stallion was all too eager to oblige.

Indie was neither embarrassed nor shocked or offended. She was fascinated. Interested. Maybe slightly uncomfortable with the high degree of all that, but not afraid to keep watching.

Wes had to clamp down on the intense sexual and intellectual connection that grew in leaps and bounds within him.

"The mare's name is Moxy and the stallion is Rocket," Wes said.

A handler held Moxy's lead shank as the stallion approached. She kicked out, but the protective leather booties on her hind feet prevented injury to the stallion.

Rocket sniffed Moxy, and then raised his head

and inhaled as he rolled his upper lip up, baring big horse teeth.

"Doesn't he like her?" Indie asked.

Wes had to hold back a laugh. Horses could be intimidating creatures, especially when they showed their teeth. They were considerably bigger than humans. But if trained right, and treated right, they were gentle herbivores.

"He likes her a lot," Wes said. "He's about to mount her."

Indie glanced at him as though doubtful.

"You'll see. His name isn't Rocket for no reason." He nodded toward the stallion.

"Oh," Indie said as she noticed the animal's genitals. "I see."

One of two of the mare's handlers lifted her foreleg with a leather strap while the other held her tail aside as the stallion approached, nostrils flaring and muscles taught. The handler held the leg to prevent the mare from kicking. The stallion mounted her, and the handler released Randi's leg.

Wes watched Indie. As he had seen this so many times, it was no shock to him. It was just business. And a deep love for his horses.

He knew the stallion had pushed the broodmare against the protective chest shield, cushioned for the mare's comfort. He knew the stallion now penetrated the mare.

Indies mouth dropped open and her eyes were big and unblinking. It never took long for the procreating stallion's tail to start flagging, indicating he had reached ejaculation.

Rocket dismounted.

Indie's mouth remained open and her eyes were still round with wonder.

Wes remained silent and unmoving, waiting for her to drift back down to Earth.

After the mare and stallion were led away, each through different doors, Indie at last turned to him, eyes still full of wonder but mouth back to normal.

"That was *amazing!"* she exclaimed.

"It always is," he said. "And if you think that was incredible, just wait till the foal is born." He grinned. That was always a miraculous thing to witness.

Indie's eyes closed as she lifted her head in awe. "I want to see that."

"You will." Wes drew her closer and held her for a moment. Her warm and happy, even content face, made him act on impulse. Slowly, he lowered his mouth to hers. Pressing his lips to hers lightly, heat shot through him. He withdrew, a little startled. She looked the way he felt as their gazes met.

Wes felt an arrow of something too powerful, too personal, and too close to his heart drive through his soul.

Chapter 12

About a week later, Indie called Detective Joyce. She had received word that the fibers from the scarf matched fibers from the crime scenes where they were found. There were also other fibers that appeared to be from vehicle carpeting. The fibers were only in certain victims' hair or on their shoes where shoes were recovered at the scenes.

"So, the victims were either wrapped in something when they were put in the vehicle or they were lying on something," Detective Joyce said.

"Depending on when the fibers got there. Was it just after they were abducted? After they were raped? In all the cases I found, the victims were murdered at the crime scene." Did the psychopath rape them somewhere and then kill them at the scene?

"Mine were killed at the scene, too," the detective said. "I'd say he raped them somewhere else and then took them to his scene of choice, where he killed them."

"With fibers in their hair and on their shoes, that suggests they were lying down, like in a trunk."

"And lying on something else. Maybe he had a mat or liner in the trunk but it didn't cover all of the carpet."

"That's a good thought," Indie said. "He may have put something down to avoid the victims collecting forensic evidence."

"A slipup on his part."

"I doubt he was worried about getting caught. He left semen in all the cases and used the same blindfold—presumably."

"He seems worried now," Detective Joyce said. "Your counterpart at DAI told me about your attack."

"Yes…" Indie recalled how terrified she had been, hating that feeling as much now as she had then.

"They all make mistakes. Forensics today is not what it was a decade ago. Their biggest problem is thinking they can outsmart us."

But they did, for the most part, in her opinion. They killed too many people before anyone could crack the case. Serial killers weren't afraid to leave evidence. Their confidence and cunning led them to evade capture. In this case, it would be the trace evidence that would help her the most. Trace evidence was difficult to control for the killer.

"I just heard the fibers from the scarf from Mya's

crime scene match those from Tessa, Cheryl and Briana," Indie told the detective.

"That's excellent news," he said.

It was excellent news. She was closer than ever to shining a spotlight on the killer. Now, if they could just get a lead on his identity...

Indie saw headlights through the office window. Wes was back from the stables. She noticed the time. It was getting late. As though on cue, her stomach growled.

"Let's keep in touch on status," she said into the phone.

"Will do. And, Indie," Detective Joyce said, "I'm honored to be working with you on this."

"Thank you. I'm happy to have the help. The last thing we want is another murder."

"Absolutely."

She ended the call and left her office.

Her office...

Since when had she began thinking of it as that?

Wes greeted Thomas, one of the guards, on his way toward the front door. Samuel had the day shift this week and Thomas kept watch at night. He must have just come back from his first patrol.

"Good evening, Mr. McCann," Thomas said. He looked a little somber.

Wes shook his hand. "Is everything all right?"

"I saw someone on your property a few minutes ago," the bodyguard said.

Just now? Wes looked around and saw nothing out of the ordinary. "Where?"

"Not anywhere that anyone should have been." He nodded toward the trees in the distance.

"Are you sure it wasn't an animal?" Wes asked. The killer could have found out who he was and where he lived. He had seen him in town the day Indie had escaped him.

"I'm sure. As I was hiking through the trees, I saw someone walking near the road. He must have seen me because he turned around and headed back toward a car. It was too dark and I was too far away to get a look at the plate, but it appeared to be similar to the car Indie saw passing the diner."

Wes sighed. "All right. I'll lock up tight tonight." Looked like he wouldn't get much sleep that evening. He'd be too worried a homicidal maniac was loose on his property.

Entering the house, he heard Indie finishing a conversation on the phone. He stopped at her office door as she stood from the desk and approached him.

"Did you talk to Thomas?" she asked.

"Just now."

"What happened?"

After quickly filling her in, he met her eyes grimly, seeing the same anxiety he felt reflected in her expression.

"Well. You up for a night of G-rated movies?" she asked.

"Sure. I was just thinking I won't be able to sleep," he said.

She walked into the living room and turned on the television while Wes went around the house checking windows and doors. He had motion detectors in the backyard and the lights in the front came on automatically as the sun set.

Back in the living room, he saw Indie had found an animated film. "What do you want for dinner?"

"A dead serial killer," she said, turning her head with a smile.

He chuckled. "I don't have a platter big enough for that."

She laughed and he saw how the joking eased her tension.

"Beef stroganoff and a salad?" he asked.

"Sounds perfect." She got up and went into the kitchen with him and together they began to prepare the meal. He felt as though this were a routine he could do every day with her.

Wes was no chef but he was particular about the kind of beef he ate. It had to be lean and it had to be tender. He seasoned some flour and lightly coated the beef tenderloin. Indie got some oil going in a fry pan and a pot of water boiling. He manned the beef while she dumped noodles into the hot water. Then she chopped some vegetables for a salad. He kept glancing over, curious to know what kind of salad she liked. Spring mix lettuce, tomatoes, green and red peppers, canned corn, black olives and feta cheese all went into the mix. She was a veggie lover. Fine by him. He wasn't a picky eater but after a long day of work he liked a dinner that would stick to his ribs.

Wes added a half loaf of French bread, not expecting her to eat any of it. It was a lot of food for a woman.

But when he sat across from her at the table, she dug right in. Her plate had almost as much food on it as his.

"How do you keep such a slender figure?" he asked.

She looked up as she stuffed in a mouthful of stroganoff. Chewing and finally swallowing, she said, "I don't eat like this all the time. I skipped lunch today."

So she was starving, too. Were they so in sync that they lived on the same wavelength or was this coincidence? He didn't care. He loved it that she could stuff her face every once in a while.

"Mmm. The meat is fantastic and so is the sauce," she said.

"My grandmother's recipe. She tenderized her meat, though. I buy it already tender."

"Grandmothers are a wonderful thing. I wish I could have spent more time with mine before she died."

Once again he was reminded of how they both had no family, none worth mentioning anyway. Sometimes Wes had contemplated trying to connect with a few of his distant cousins but they lived so far away he never followed through.

"Do you like to cook?" she asked.

"Only when the end result is going to be delicious."

She smiled and laughed as she forked another creamy bite.

"Do you?"

"Only when the end result is going to be delicious."

He chuckled. "What comes to mind as one of those dishes?"

"Copycat Big Mac recipe and French fries, except I don't have that extra piece of bread. It's still really fattening but so juicy and good."

"Okay, that's dinner on Sunday."

"Deal. We have a few days to work off the calories from this." She looked at him happily and with a light in her eyes he thought was attraction or a little flirtation.

It caused a reaction in him he had no control over. Her eyes changed in an instant and her smile faded as the moment warmed.

The sound of gunfire outside wiped away any brewing sexual desire. Wes went to grab his rifle and Indie removed her pistol, not having removed her gun belt yet.

"Call 911!" she yelled, going for the door.

"Indie, don't go out there!" Wes took hold of her arm, making her turn to face him. "Wait for the guard to come in."

She didn't argue, but she went to the office and, keeping the lights off, peered through the blinds. Wes followed, looking over her head. He didn't see the guard at first but then spotted him running down the drive and disappearing from view when he left the perimeter of outdoor lighting.

Wes took out his cell phone and dial 911, telling the dispatcher they had an armed intruder.

More gunshots popped in the night. Then a man appeared in the outdoor lighting. He was running toward the house, with Thomas chasing him from behind. The intruder took cover behind a tree in Wes's front yard and began firing. Thomas had no protective cover.

"I've got to help him!" Indie said, flinching as they both watched him get shot and go down. She moved away from the window.

"Our guard was just shot," Wes told the dispatcher.

He followed Indie to the front door. Outside, she began firing at the intruder. Wes raised his rifle and commenced doing the same.

The intruder ran into the trees. Indie started to go after him, but Wes stopped her again.

"The police will be here soon," he reminded her.

"That killer will get away by then." She tugged at his hold on her.

"You aren't a cop anymore, Indie, you're a private detective."

"A PI who knows how to chase a suspect," she said. "And I'm a good shot."

He released her. "I'm sorry. I feel protective of you." Because he had strong feelings for her. He didn't say as much but he saw her recognize the affliction.

She looked toward the trees. "He's long gone by now anyway. We need to see if Thomas is all right."

Wes ran ahead of her toward the bodyguard, who stirred on the ground in the driveway. He searched the vicinity with his rifle, ready to fire.

"Thomas?" Indie crouched beside him.

He sat up holding his right shoulder. "I'm all right. Did he get away?"

"Yes."

Wes helped Thomas to his feet. He feared the killer was still lurking and wanted to get all of them somewhere safer.

At last they reached the house, where he put Thomas on a chair in the entry. Indie had kept guard, moving backward with her gun ready. Now she went into the bathroom to retrieve a towel, pressing it to Thomas's wound. He tipped his head back, eyes droopy. He was fading fast.

"Stay with us," she said urgently.

Thomas looked at her and blinked a few times, clearly fighting.

"That's it, Thomas. You're going to be all right. Help is on the way." She glanced up at Wes, who looked at her from the front door, where he kept vigilance.

At last the sound of sirens grew louder.

A sheriff's SUV drove up the driveway first, followed by an unmarked car and two police cars. Then finally, a firetruck and an ambulance arrived.

The sheriff approached the house and Indie stepped outside.

"He went that way." She pointed.

"We'll check it out," one of the police officers said, and two of them went running toward the trees.

Wes let the sheriff and another man he had never seen before inside. Behind him he saw the paramedics race up. Everyone got out of the way so they could attend to Thomas.

"Mr. McCann, this is Detective Michael Radcliff. He's the primary contact for the investigation on Mya's murder." The sheriff nodded toward Indie, then turned back to Wes. "Radcliff's been in close contact with Kadin Tandy on this case, who appointed Indiana Deboe to provide assistance in solving this most disturbing murder."

"I'm aware of that," Wes said.

"What you may not be aware of is that Kadin has promised highly restrictive protocols in place for all his detectives to follow," the detective interjected, looking at Indie.

Wes glanced at her, who gave him a look that said the announcement fell flat for her. She would do whatever she had to do to solve a case, to bring a criminal to justice. There were laws she couldn't break and evidence had to be handled properly, but that didn't get in the way of her tenacity.

"We work under the auspices of whoever is officially in charge of the cases we are independently hired to work," she said simply.

As Detective Radcliff's mouth curved in a self-serving but subtle smile, Wes realized Indie and her famous boss had the local law enforcement under some kind of spell. The elite agency must adhere to stringent confidentiality protocols. Convincing protocols, but to solve some of the cases they worked took tactics that must breach at least some laws. Clearly those breaches never came to light. The number one priority was the victim and their families. And preserving evidence, of course. No cutting corners there…

Wes found himself feeling new respect for Kadin Tandy. He and his team of bold detectives virtually handed murderers of cold cases over to law enforcement, with stellar expertise.

The paramedics took Thomas away and the policemen returned to take their statements. All the while Detective Radcliff waited and listened patiently. He was a quiet man. Maybe his reserve was even calculated. But he hadn't solved the Berry case, so he must not be very competent, unless his department didn't provide him the resources DAI could afford. Surely he must know that, and probably his boss did as well.

After the others left, Detective Radcliff finally came to life. He had stayed silent while the sheriff spoke with them and Thomas was taken away.

"We have a lot to discuss," he said, sounding not very pleased. "I spoke with Kadin and there seems to be some significant developments on the case."

"Coffee?" Indie offered.

He softened somewhat. "Yes, creamer if you have it."

"We do," Wes said, "and I'll get it. You two get to work."

She took the detective to her office, sat at her desk and invited him to move a chair next to her so he could see her computer.

He seemed to like that. Transparency.

"You must not know Kadin Tandy very well," she said.

"I do know him. He's a smooth talker."

"When he wants a case solved, yes. His intention is to have a respectable and professional relationship with all law enforcement. But make no mistake. He only cares about the victims." She sent him a direct look.

Detective Radcliff's eyes grew less defensive. "He did tell me about his daughter."

"Kadin would never do anything to compromise evidence, but he gives all of his private investigators free rein to ferret out the killers," she said. "You have my word that the chain of evidence will not be broken. Nor will I ever reveal details of the case to anyone not in law enforcement working the case. Which is why I'm about to share what Wes and I recently learned."

Wes entered the office and delivered the coffee, then turned and left, closing the door behind him.

Indie appreciated his professionalism as well as his care in treating the handling of this case with the detective in charge.

She went through a lengthy narrative of what Detective Joyce and she had discussed, paying particular attention and detail to why they both believed the murders were linked.

Radcliff examined her notes and digested all the information. Then he looked at her.

"This is significant," he said.

She nodded. "Yes. I'll send you everything I have."

"Thanks. With your composite sketch of the suspect, we could crack this case."

Indie was surprised at his level of enthusiasm. She knew the detective to be professional but he had to feel threatened by the weight of an agency like DAI breathing over his case.

Perhaps things weren't so hostile now that he knew she had no intention of leaving him in the dust.

"We will solve this case," she said. "We will catch this serial killer."

"Your confidence is encouraging," Radcliff said. "What can I do to help?"

"Keep doing what you're doing. Provide resources when necessary and meet with me to keep up on status. I'll be sure to let your office process any evidence, as usual, and funnel reports to you as things progress. Your case file will, of course be the official one."

He nodded. "I have to admit, I was skeptical at first, having a PI take over the investigation. But now I can see it was not only necessary, but a blessing."

Indie was accustomed to hearing accolades like this. She smiled amicably. She also understood egos were involved. "We couldn't do it without detectives like you."

He smiled appreciatively and stood. "I look forward to working with you, Ms. Deboe."

"Please, it's Indie." She shook his hand.

She let him out of her office and then the front door. Then she turned to the house and went to find Wes, looking forward to sharing the rest of the evening with him. She could use the excuse that it was her good spirits, but that would be a lie. She liked being with him. It seemed she liked that more and more. While a cautionary thought tried to manifest into something bigger, she wasn't going to let that ruin her night.

"How'd it go?" Wes handed her a glass of red wine, already knowing by the look on her face—the slight, upward turn of her mouth, the sweet glow in her eyes—that things had gone well.

Looking up from the couch where she sat, she took the wine. "Great. I think he finally trusts us now."

By *us* she meant her prestigious agency. "Well, a man would have to blind and dumb not to utilize the might of your boss."

"Yes, but sometimes I get tired of hearing that. What we do isn't about the fame. It's about the victims."

He knew she cared deeply about the victims and could relate to them on a personal level. It was one of the things that attracted him to her. She had heart, real heart. "I know, but…it's still inspiring. DAI is famous because they do what they do *for* the victims."

Her mouth curved up into a soft smile. "Thanks, Wes."

As she sipped, her gaze roamed around the room that didn't really define him. Not yet. It needed a family's touch.

"A woman would have to be blind and dumb not

to realize what a strong and successful rancher you are," she said with a teasing smile.

At first he thought the positivity of her meeting with the detective had loosened her tongue. But his instinct and the warmth in her eyes conveyed honesty.

"You've always liked ranchers?" he asked, sitting next to her.

"No. I didn't know how much until I met you."

He felt as though they were both testing each other. Saying things they most likely meant but veiling it with teasing banter.

"What kind of men attracted you before you met me?" he asked.

"Well…" She seemed to think about that for a minute. "I thought I knew before I met my ex-husband and then Russ. Tall. Handsome. Nice butt. Wants a family. I didn't focus on what made them tick."

"What would you like to make them tick?" he quipped, trying to keep it light.

While she lowered her head in another long contemplation, Wes wondered about her marriage and her relationship with Russ. She had been so evasive about that. The end of her marriage and her relationship with the man seemed to have happened close together. He had no concrete information supporting that but the way she talked about both of them felt one and the same, as though both the man she married and the boyfriend after that had too many similarities. And he knew she hadn't dated seriously since.

"Nicholas Nickleby," she said at last.

"From the Dickens novel?" he asked.

She nodded. "A gentleman but manly. Someone who stands for honor." Her eyes moved upward as though reaching for thought. "Someone…secure with himself."

Wes sensed her sincerity and faltered a little. "I'm not that pure." He was secure with himself but not with relationships… Who knew how they could end up? "And I suspect, neither are you."

They both came from flawed experiences. Their innocence was lost long ago.

"Someone is bound to come along for both of us and we'll overcome," she said.

She left him thinking why not them? But he couldn't explain why her marriage and then her relationship with Russ bothered him. He supposed after a terrible marriage she'd be reluctant to see anyone else. So, why had she?

"How did you meet Russ?" he asked.

She looked perplexed that he had asked such a personal question. Then closed off as she always did when he brought up her past loves.

After a few long seconds, she looked at him and said, "He was the policeman who helped me get away from Cole."

Get away? He was surprised she'd revealed that detail.

"Cole was abusive," she said, abrupt and full of discomfort.

Now he knew why she was so reluctant to discuss her past. So many questions bombarded him. "Wait. What? What happened?"

Indie stood from the couch and walked away, folding her arms. This was obviously a difficult subject for her and he had to be careful not to rush her or infringe on her emotional boundaries. But he really wanted to know. He *needed* to know.

He stood and went to stand just behind her. Then reached out and gently touched her shoulder.

Turning, she lifted her head and met his eyes. She looked lost and tortured, likely with terrible memories. He could feel her vulnerability and wanted only to be here for her, to somehow give her comfort, if not closure to what had to come with awful aftereffects.

"He was a weak man," she said. "Controlling. Jealous. I was independent and free when I met him but he stripped all of that away from me. I had to live under his rule or suffer beatings. I had no friends. I didn't go anywhere other than the grocery store. I had to order my wardrobe online. Those deliveries were my savior and my outlet."

Wes felt poleaxed. He would have never guessed. Indie was the strongest woman he'd ever met. That she would be in a situation where she was so held down confounded him.

"Weren't you a cop by then?" he asked.

"Yes, and then a detective. The thing you have to understand is Cole was a violent man. He duped me when we first met and married. He was not the same person at all. There was no resemblance whatsoever. He turned into a monster. I called 911 once and nearly didn't survive what he did to me after that. He went to jail but was out in no time. I wasn't dead, after all.

Just beaten. Russ was one of the responding officers. He kept in touch with me after that. Helped me get a restraining order. That didn't work, though."

"Did you leave him?" he asked.

"No, I put all of his things in the yard and he picked them up and moved somewhere. Russ was there with me when he moved his things."

"What happened after that?" Wes asked.

"I went to work for Kadin. He made sure Cole understood if he ever came within a hundred miles of me, he'd be a dead man."

"And Russ?"

"We were together for a while. But then it ended."

"What happened?" he asked. The subject of Russ seemed to have taken a sour turn for her.

"It just…didn't work out. I wasn't ready for a new relationship."

Wes stared at her, unable to shake the feeling that she was being deliberately vague. *Again.* She had gone through hell with her ex-husband. He believed she had been vulnerable, but what had drawn her to the man other than his support during a rough time? And why had she ended the relationship? Most of all, what was her reason for not wanting to discuss Russ? He understood her hesitancy about Cole, but why Russ?

Chapter 13

Three a.m. and Indie still couldn't sleep. She kept going over and over again their conversation about Cole and Russ. It had been difficult for her to tell Wes about Cole, but she felt good about doing so. However, Russ was another story altogether. Those two relationships had altered her course in life. Ruined her optimism. Made her want to isolate. Be alone. Pave her own way and not depend on anyone other than herself to survive.

Yes, she had contemplated the possibility of meeting a man she could trust, but always the threatening afterthoughts came. She was afraid to try again. Plain and simple.

Indie sensed Wes's distrust and didn't blame him. She had been secretive about her life. But he didn't

understand. He wasn't a woman and he had never
been abused, verbally or physically. Arguably, Charlotte may have verbally abused him, given her distaste
for ranching. Wes was a strong man, so the caustic
words likely hadn't impacted him. Only the disappointment of marrying the wrong woman had. He
was distrustful like her, but for very different reasons. Reasons that could send Indie into another bad
downward spiral.

When Wes had questioned her about Russ, she had
actually felt she could tell all. Had wanted to, in fact,
and her heart had tugged her in that direction. But old
insecurities had intervened. It had begun with bad relationships with men. Losing her family compounded
her emotional vulnerability. Seeking comfort from
others had not proved beneficial for her since then.
Life's circumstances and her decisions had failed her.

She wanted so badly to open herself to Wes. Everything in her said he was nothing like Cole, that
he would never hurt her, but she had thought the
same about Cole. She couldn't take the chance. Even
if it meant losing a good thing. Wariness and self-
preservation overruled.

A soft knock on her partially open door awakened
her weary head.

Wes pushed the door open. "Come sleep with me,
Indie. There's no point in us being alone."

His offer pierced her depressing thoughts.

"Come on. We both know we're lonely and looking
for…something we've not had since we were kids."

His candid words of truth broke her barriers. A

powerful wave of relief washed through her. A night of sleeplessness with nothing to accompany her but exactly what he had named—loneliness—was far more unpalatable than a night spent next to another human being who had experienced loss similar to hers.

She could not resist his olive branch. At least not tonight…

Drawing the covers off her, she stood, her knee-length, cream-colored nightie faithfully falling to cover her where she felt secure.

Wes held his hand out to her and she took it, so tired and grateful for this lifeline.

He had already pulled back the covers on his bed. Indie crawled onto the cool, soft sheets and felt peace wash over her. She would sleep next to him tonight…

Wes put the blankets over her, gentle and slow. She saw his eyes in the dimness of the bedroom and they reached into her soul. Two kindred spirits randomly thrown together. Indie let the warmth and love flood her. He closed his eyes briefly, as though feeling the same as her, and then straightened and went to his side of the bed.

Indie lay on her back, yearning for human closeness. *His* closeness. She was aroused but her immediate need was for that contact with a man who wouldn't demand more than comfort.

Wes opened his arm to her. "Get over here."

She smiled and curled up next to him, immeasurable satisfaction swarming around her heart. She closed her eyes, reveling in the feeling. This was exactly what she needed right now.

He wrapped his arm around her. "Let's just be like this for tonight."

Oh. Had he read her that accurately or did he feel the same as her? Her gut said the latter.

"Yes," she said, her voice sounding soft and drowsy. She rested her hand on his chest. Nothing felt righter.

She basked in the moment, his warm body next to her, no demand for sex, just companionship. She wanted him to know how much this meant to her.

"Wes?" she began.

"Yes?"

His deep, sleepy and masculine voice arrowed into her heart. "Thank you."

"For what?"

She knew he didn't have to ask. But he needed her to say it.

"For being you." After she said that, she drifted off into sweet oblivion.

Wes woke to a ringing phone. The next thing he became aware of was Indie's slender and sexy body pressed against him. Her breasts pressed to his chest, and her arm and leg draped across him. Her hair fell over his arm that supported her head. Good Lord. Her need for closeness had nearly done him in last night. Turning his head, he saw her face completely relaxed in deep sleep. When was the last time she had slept like this? He had slept well, too, but her nearness had tested every bit of his restraint. He'd had to clamp off every male instinct to roll her on her back and go to the next level. Thank goodness she hadn't been aware of how hard he had been.

The ringing sounded again.

Indie stirred. Then moaned.

"It's yours," he said. She was going to make him hard again if she kept making that sound.

Indie had taken to sleeping with her phone by the bed in case something broke in the case. Judging from the hour, something must have.

Lifting her head, she looked at him sleepily, then down his body, clearly registering their positions. Waking fully, she rolled and picked up her phone and pressed the speaker.

"Deboe."

"Detective," a man's voice said. "I'm Ethan Campbell from the El Paso Police Department, homicide division."

Indie sat up on the bed. "Yes, Detective Campbell. What can I do for you?"

Wes sat up, too, leaning against the headboard, his erection officially gone with the gravity of the call, and what he suspected it would entail.

"I apologize for the early hour, but I figured you would want to know what I recently uncovered." After a brief pause he said, "I believe I have information on your Mya Berry case."

"All right. You've definitely got my attention." Wes saw Indie take her lower lip between her teeth, anxious and waiting to hear what the man had to say.

"A female bartender got off work after closing time and I believe a man was waiting for her and followed her home. This seems to be a pattern. She was taken as soon as she got out of her car—never made it into her house. She didn't know him, so this was a random attack. After abducting her outside her car, he took her to a cemetery, where she was assaulted. She escaped from her wrist binding and fought him when he got the knife out. Kicked him where it counts and ran to a road, where someone stopped and helped her."

With each sentence, the man pinged on everything that had happened to Mya, except for her murder.

"She survived?" Indie asked, needing confirmation.

"Yes."

"Was she blindfolded?"

"Yes," the detective confirmed. "The perp used a scarf during the attack. I have fiber analyses being processed."

Indie turned to Wes, eyes alert and full of enthusiasm. "She lived." She smiled, clearly elated about that, but of course, not minimizing what the victim must have gone through. And Wes knew this was a huge break in the case. The scarf could link the killer to other murders, along with other DNA evidence.

"Yes. Thank goodness for that," Campbell said, "Which makes this case incredibly important. She was able to identify him."

That bombshell hit Indie with explosive significance. Wes heard her let out a long breath. This kept getting better and better.

"His name is Aaron Bennett. He was arrested on attempted rape charges several years ago, prior to any of the cases you've linked together. I spoke with Detective Radcliff before calling you. He said he was able to talk with some of Mya's coworkers and she was wearing a scarf the day she was murdered."

Indie took a few moments before saying, "Who's handing the chain of evidence?"

"Actually, now the FBI. The murders crossed state lines. We have proof of that. There's an agent who's been informed of all the developments. He has your contact information."

Wes watched Indie's eyes close and then open, absorbing this turn of events.

"This man attacked me. He abducted me," she said. "He's killed way too many women as it is. He would have killed me if he had the chance."

And done God knows what else to her. Wes hated that thought.

"Yes. And on that note, you're personally involved in this now, Ms. Deboe. Are you concerned you won't have the lead anymore?"

"No. I'm a PI. I want to be *professionally* involved." Wes recognized she wanted to be the one to take this sicko down. Now the FBI was involved. She didn't unwelcome it, but she wanted to be an integral part of the fight.

After several seconds, Campbell said, "You will be. The FBI's biggest concern is the surviving witness…and you."

Indie turned and met Wes's eyes and he saw her

fear and doubt. For a killer like this, if he felt threatened, he'd start eliminating possible witnesses. Indie was one. The assault victim was another.

"I've emailed you a photo of Aaron. Can you tell me if he's the same man who abducted you?" Campbell asked.

"Yes. Give me a few moments."

Indie got off the bed and Wes watched her scurry in her knee-length nightie to the dresser. She opened her laptop. After booting up, she navigated with her mouse.

Then, she grew very still. Wes could see part of her screen. An image of a dark-haired man with dead brown eyes masked by a smile appeared. Eerie. Who smiled for a mug shot?

Her breathing quickened with apprehension. "That's him."

"You're sure?" Campbell asked.

"Yes. Absolutely. That's him." She put her hand over her mouth and sort of stumbled back a step.

Wes got up and went to her, putting his hands on her shoulders.

"Okay. Now all we need to do is find him. The last intel we have on him is he was fired from his job at a convenience store near the abandoned cabin where he took you. Then he was evicted from his apartment. We are pretty sure he was living in the abandoned cabin. We lost his trail from there."

Indie turned to face Wes, who slipped his arms around her loosely. "I'll see what I can dig up on him."

"Good. I'll send over what I have on the latest victim," he said.

After disconnecting, she fell into sort of a daze. A thousand thoughts must be racing through her right now. And he also sensed a little disconcertion. Aaron Bennet had abducted her and would have killed her had she not escaped. He was an extremely dangerous man.

Wes would never be able to comprehend how anyone could do the things that man had done to all those women. What made someone go so far over an edge like that? Even perverse sexual fantasies didn't seem enough to make a man crack apart like that. It was so sickening.

Indie's hands came to rest on his chest, distracting his morbid thoughts. She had come out of her daze and now looked up at him. He became as aware as she must be of how close they were...and the warmth of the connection that sparked just now.

"I'm so glad you're here during all of this," she whispered.

He knew she meant she was grateful to have someone near her, after her abduction. She was not the kind of woman who felt weakness, and now that she experienced that, she didn't know how to deal with it. As he had surmised before this.

Not sure how to address her in this moment, he said, "It's okay to feel vulnerable, Indie. It's also okay to depend on others when you need them."

Their faces were close, hers tipped up to his, and

her eyes met his in heartfelt sincerity. "How can you say that when you've had losses and disappointments, too?"

"I couldn't have said it before I met you," he said.

She blinked slowly as she comprehended the meaning of that.

Drawn in by her beauty and her transparency, Wes lowered his head and kissed her. He simply pressed his lips to hers, feeling her warmth and smelling her sweet scent.

She slid her hands up his chest and around to the back of his neck and shoulder. The kiss deepened with the swell of enamored emotion. Wes could not process this mysterious connection he had with her. What made him so into her? She was smart. Beautiful. Capable. All of those words came to him until he fell into the wonder of the love they created just now.

He heard her breathing and became aware of his own. If this continued, they'd be in bed.

She broke away first, heated eyes meeting his. Lord, how he wanted her. He wanted her in a way that went far beyond sexual.

Stepping back, she covered her lips with three fingers, then turned and walked away.

He was glad she had done that. She'd be his undoing if this went any further than it already had. He feared she was already his undoing.

"I'm sorry," she said as she half turned her head back to him.

Sorry? He was the one who had kissed her. "I think we both just need some time."

She nodded and he saw her appreciation in the glow of her pretty blue eyes.

Chapter 14

Throughout the next day, Indie had trouble with the potency of her kiss with Wes. In the morning, she had awkwardly entered the kitchen, where he had already prepared coffee. This thing between them kept mushrooming into something out of control. And way too emotionally captivating than she felt comfortable facing.

They had avoided each other easily enough the rest of the day, she working in her office and he going out on the ranch. Right now, he drove with her to where Juliet Williams, the surviving victim, was staying with her parents while she recovered from her traumatic ordeal. Indie had read all that Detective Campbell had sent her. Juliet worked at an upscale restaurant and pub, from where she had taken time off to heal.

Indie parked across the street from a pale blue bungalow-style house with white trim. After ten in the evening, the outside lights were on and all the windows were dark. Stone pillars supported the covered front porch. It was a nice, well-maintained home in a middle-class neighborhood. Juliet appeared to come from a decent family. Indie hoped she had the support she needed during this difficult time.

Driving farther up the street, she made a U-turn on the empty street and found an inconspicuous place to park off to the side. She turned off the headlights. They'd wait here to see if Aaron made any appearance.

"Do you do this often?" Wes asked.

"All night stakeouts?" She glanced back at the cooler and then at the two thermoses of coffee in the console. "Not often but I do them."

"Do you have trouble staying awake?"

"Sometimes. Coffee helps. So does the purpose," she said. Many times these stakeouts led to arrests. It had been a few days since Juliet's attack, about the right amount of time before Indie would expect Aaron to strike.

Wes looked over at her. "You think he'll try to go after her?"

"If he's caught, she's a witness who can put him in prison, possibly with a death penalty if all the DNA matches." The DNA evidence would likely be enough for a conviction, but there was nothing more powerful than the testimony of a surviving victim.

"Maybe we should follow Juliet wherever she goes for a while," Wes suggested.

"When I spoke with Campbell this morning, he said her mother told him she hasn't left the house at all and doesn't want to."

Wes sighed sympathetically. "That poor woman."

"She's lucky to be alive," Indie said. "But yes, what woman wouldn't have trouble overcoming an attack like that? It will take time."

The street was quiet and void of cars or people. Most everyone was probably home and asleep by now.

"I can see why you do what you do," he said. "Helping people. Saving lives."

Most of the time she didn't save lives. She brought those who took them to justice. But Indie understood his meaning. It was her background that had driven her down this course in life.

"It has its moments," she admitted, turning to look at him with a slight smile. It was so easy to talk to him.

He smiled back in similar fashion and the energy flared between them. Indie was beginning to become accustomed to it…or, rather, she was giving up on fighting this magnetic pull between them.

Wes was the first to turn away. He bent his head slightly with a single, breathy laugh, if one could call it that. More like a wry exhale.

"Happens every time," he said, lifting his head. He tilted it slightly, then looked at her again. *So sexy.*

She thought she knew what he meant but sent him a question with her eyes.

"That spark," he said. "I can't control it…can you?"

Now she was the one to let out a wry breath. "No." The way he looked at her and where this was leading raised her defenses. It didn't help that she had thought the same thing earlier.

"Maybe it's time we talked about that."

What could they say that would change anything? "What do you want to talk about?"

"Well, for one, why does it keep happening?"

Indie wished she knew. Thinking about that now, she would say it was his attractiveness that had elicited the fiery reaction, at least initially, but then something else had come into play. Him as a man.

"I don't know, but one of the first things that struck me was that you were alone at that party like me," she said.

"Yes. I noticed that about you, too," he said. "And then we hit it off."

"The banter." She laughed softly. "Yes."

"When Julien came to the table, my interest in you went way up," he said.

Surprised by his candor, Indie began to wonder if he had a purpose for bringing this up.

"I don't mean to sound sexist, but you were so beautiful I didn't expect you to be a detective," he said. "I would have never guessed."

He had thought she was beautiful? "What would you have guessed?"

"Model. Heiress."

That sort of hurt. "That sounds so vacuous. No offense to models and heiresses, but…" That so did not fit her.

"I wasn't thinking those particular descriptors at the time, but I did think you belonged on the bow of a yacht."

Indie laughed harder. "I had you pegged for a rancher the instant I saw you."

He nodded. "The hat and the others in attendance?"

She nodded back, still smiling.

"I think it was more than physical attraction," he said. "I think we had some kind of kindred connection."

"Loneliness?" She joked, but then, not really. Indie could not argue there had been more than physical attraction, but what was he getting at? "Wes…is there something you want to ask me?"

He grinned. "That's another kindred connection we have. You're so in tune with me."

She angled her head in reprimand. This was getting way too deep for her. She began to feel cornered.

"If it weren't for your murder case, what do you think would have happened between us?" he asked, hedging.

"That's kind of a broad question," she said, admitting to herself she was also hedging. What *would* have happened?

"You wouldn't have followed me home," she said.

"I would have thought about you for weeks. I might have even asked Julien for your number."

He would have? She had made that much of an impression on him?

"You know I coerced you to come and stay with me more for personal reasons, right?" he asked.

He had been interested in her romantically, even though technically he had still been married. Granted, after a while, he had told her once he met her he had some epiphanies regarding his ex-wife, but he had been *married*. She had a cardinal rule to never get involved with a married man.

"Yes, and I went with you for the same reasons," she said, not proud of herself. She had to be honest, however.

Maybe it was good they were having this talk. They needed to come to some understanding.

They shared long seconds where they each kept staring at each other. This wasn't an easy topic for either of them.

"How do you view our relationship?" he finally asked.

Relationship.

"Is that what this is?" she asked. Her stomach churned with nerves. Memories of her ex-husband swirled through her mind.

"It is to me," Wes said. "What I need to know is if you'll still be with me after Aaron is captured."

Her stomach flopped again, this time with excitement mixed in. "Um…i-is that what you want?"

"I want to see if we have something that will last," he said. His sincerity radiated across the car to her.

"Wes… I…" She did not know what to say. "A-aren't you afraid of making the same mistake you made with Charlotte?"

"Jumping into another relationship too soon? Yes. Absolutely. But what if this is worth the risk?"

She couldn't find a single word to say. Indecision rendered her at a loss. "We haven't known each other very long. It is too soon to be contemplating a future together."

"I have never felt this way about any other woman in my entire life. How do you feel?"

"Do we have to talk about this now?" Indie glanced around to look for signs of Aaron. She needed to focus on something other than a man who turned her on as much as Wes did.

"Yes, and that is why. You're still afraid to let yourself go with a man. You're afraid to open your heart. Except, what you haven't admitted is you already have despite the fact that you fight it. That's why I need to talk about this now. I have to do what's best for myself here. This is getting too serious for me."

He had a very good point, of course. She didn't want to hurt him any more than he wanted to be hurt.

Indie propped her elbow on the door handle and put her forehead into her hand. How could she respond to this? Wes not only deserved to know how she felt, but he needed to know if she was willing to keep seeing him after the case was solved.

At last, she raised her head and looked at him. "I

haven't felt like this with any other man, either. The thing is, I don't know how I feel. I can't put it into words. And you're right. I am afraid to open my heart. One thing I have learned is the future is unpredictable. I don't do well with unpredictable."

"I am not the same as your ex-husband. What you see is who I am. I have no reason to waste my energy trying to fool you into believing I'm anything else."

"It's more than that."

"Your family? Death? Loss? That's life, Indie. It's terrible that you had so much taken from you, but you can't stop living your life out of fear."

She met his eyes and believed every word he said, but there was a deeper spot in her soul that made her resist.

"I do live my life," she said.

"You work. You're alone otherwise. You can't keep going on like that."

Indie sighed. It wasn't that she didn't want someone in her life. She had gotten so accustomed to being alone and working that the routine had settled in. Work, get home late, sleep, then start the next day. The only time she took a weekend off was when she had plans, and even then sometimes those plans were interrupted by work. She felt comfortable working. That gave her security. Funny, she had never considered that before.

"Let me ask you this way," Wes said. "Do you think you will ever be able to trust me enough to let me in?"

She tried to organize her thoughts on her feelings

and, as always, came up with jumbled-up confusion. "I don't know. When my family was killed, all I knew about love was destroyed. I had to learn how to fend for myself. I had to learn to be alone. It altered me. And then Cole…"

Cole had shattered any hope or belief or faith she had in love. So had a few others that had come after him.

"After a few years away from Cole, I decided it would be best to find someone to live with, a companion. Not hold out for true love. Honestly, I am not sure I still believe true love exists."

She met Wes's eyes, silently pleading with him to understand.

"I feel like it can with us," he said. "I used to be like you, pessimistic, cynical, and pretty much resigned to the fact that I'd never find a woman who loved me for me. But then I met you. You changed everything."

"What are you saying?" Was he trying to tell her he loved her? She'd be scared if he did.

"Exactly what I've already said. "You could be that woman, Indie. If you just gave me a chance and trusted me."

With her heart, he was saying. The concept was so foreign to her. She felt safe not trusting men. She did not feel safe with the suggestion that she trust Wes. Feeling anxiety rear up inside her, Indie turned to the street.

"At least try, okay?" he coaxed.

She turned to him. "I can't promise you anything,

but I will try." Hoping he knew how difficult that would be for her, she withdrew into work mode. Work would ease her anxiousness.

Yet again she thought of how easy it was for her to fall into that protective routine. Self-protection. But what harm would come to her if she really did try to open up to Wes? Her instinct said he was a good man who wouldn't betray her. But she had done that with Cole and he'd turned out to be a disaster. A persistent voice emerged in her mind, reminding her she had been young when she met Cole. She wasn't young anymore, not naive. Maybe what she really needed to do was trust herself.

Although Wes was glad he had broached the sensitive subject of what happened next with Indie, he was filled with foreboding. She seemed so damaged that maybe she would never be able to trust any man. She'd wind up with someone she didn't love. A friend. While that definitely worked for a lot of people, he and Indie had a real chance at true love. She might say she wasn't sure it existed, and before meeting her, Wes would have said the same thing, but he was no fool. What they had was worth pursuing.

They had given up at about 4 a.m. and slept late this morning. Now they were back on the street near Juliet's parents' house. It was around two in the morning and still no sign of Aaron.

Wes kept the conversation light, giving Indie time to absorb all they had discussed. She hadn't been very vocal, so he knew she was thinking. Good. *Keep thinking, Indie.* She was a smart woman. She'd realize what they had wasn't something either one of them should walk away from. Screw the past. He was willing to dive bravely into an uncertain future if she was.

"I see something," she said.

Wes searched the darkness, illuminated only by streetlights and the outdoor lighting of houses. Then he spotted a figure moving at the edge of the front yard of the bungalow.

"It looks like Aaron's size," she murmured. "Let's follow him."

They got out and carefully approached, seeing Aaron slip alongside the house. Indie led the way there and they crept silently to the back.

The intruder went from window to window, testing the locks and only going to the basement windows. At the back door, he peered inside.

"What's happening?" Wes whispered into her ear.

"He's looking for a way in."

"Maybe we should call the cops."

"Wait a minute. He's going around to the other side." Indie stepped into the backyard and crossed to the other side.

Wes caught a glimpse of Aaron walking to the front. He hurried there and saw him head toward the sidewalk.

"He's leaving," Indie said.

They hurried to the car and got in. She drove down the street and saw another car start up and begin driving ahead of them. It wasn't a black Charger. It was a green Subaru.

"That must be him," Wes said.

Indie nodded in agreement.

There were no other cars on the street and neither of them could see any sign of someone walking.

"We'll follow him," she said. "Maybe he'll lead us to where he's staying. Then we can call the police so they can make an arrest and get a search warrant."

"I'll write down the plate number." Wes dug into the glove compartment and found a pen.

Indie felt around inside her purse and handed him a small notebook.

He took it and she returned her attention to the road and the green Subaru.

Wes wished they could confirm it was Aaron, but getting too close might alert the man he was being tailed.

The Subaru turned a right corner. Indie did the same.

She then retrieved her pistol from the console between the seats, keeping the safety on but resting it on top of the lid to the console.

Wes noticed, and looked from the gun to her face.

"There's something sexy about you with a gun," he said.

Indie glanced at him, looking surprised he'd made a comment like that.

"You're a woman of action," he said with a grin.

She smiled.

Here they were following a serial killer and he was telling her she was sexy.

About another two or three miles down the road,

which headed into a more residential area, the Subaru made another right. In this area of the city, there were a lot of apartment buildings and older homes.

Ahead, the Subaru made a left. Staying far back without losing the ability to track where the driver was going, Indie followed. As soon as she did, the Subaru sped up. The driver knew he was being followed.

Wes debated engaging in a chase.

He doubted Aaron would lead them to his hideout. In fact, he knew he wouldn't. He would try to outrun them or maybe even engage in gunfire.

Indie pulled over to the side of the road, obviously agreeing.

"He made us. Now I want to make sure he doesn't decide to come after us. Or Juliet—again." She turned around on the street and began driving back toward the direction of Juliet's parents' home.

Once there, Indie parked where she had before. After they'd waited an hour, the sun began to glow on the horizon.

She yawned.

"Let's call it a night," Wes said. "He probably won't show during the day." And he was looking forward to getting her back to his ranch.

She needed some sleep, and so did Wes. She started the engine and began driving back toward the ranch.

They didn't talk, a testament to their weariness. Indie drove out of the town and entered the country roads he had grown to love so much. He began to wonder if she would prefer to be alone tonight. He wanted to be close to her. To wake up with him. To feel…part of a union. A lasting one.

Headlights caught his eye in the passenger side mirror. He watched the vehicle a while, seeing the car turn when Indie did. In the increasing light of dawn, he could make out the type of car it was. A black Charger.

"He's behind us," he said.

"I saw that."

The Charger sped up and came up right behind them. Aaron began firing through his open window, aiming not for them but for the rear tire. The tire blew and Indie swerved before coming to a stop.

Wes had brought his shotgun and got out of the car and start firing at the driver of the Charger.

The tires of Aaron's car squealed as he backed up in a real hurry. Then he spun his car around and raced away. He would have attempted to kill them once he forced them to stop.

Indie looked over at Wes from over the hood. He could see her apprehension.

"Let's change the tire and get home," he said.

Yes, they needed to get home. Together.

Chapter 15

Kadin sent more security forces to Wes's ranch. Wes had learned from Indie that the new guards were elite mercenaries, once employed by one of the largest international executive security companies, men who had extensive Special Forces background but no longer had a taste for supersecret missions that required staunch discipline.

Wes wondered if they bowed down to any discipline anymore. The more he learned of Indie's employer, the more he realized following the law wasn't always the number one priority.

There were four of them, all formidable sizes that rivaled Wes's, and each one probably a bit beefier than him and definitely trained in combat. But Wes was no stranger to hard work and defending what was his. He knew his weaponry. He had a lot of live-stock to protect.

If Aaron decided to attack the ranch, he would surely meet his death. Wes felt confident Indie was safe. Who wouldn't, with Dark Alley Investigators' finest surrounding them?

Three of the mercenaries patrolled the property. One stayed close to the house. Organizing this took a matter of hours. He and Indie hadn't slept yet. They had eaten, but the drama lingered.

Aaron might not strike tonight, or here at the ranch, but he'd take his time to find vulnerability. Access. Even the toughest ex-military men might not be able to outsmart a serial killer.

Feet up on a recliner, Wes closed his eyes, hoping he could catch some sleep. He had closed all his light-blocking blinds. He listened to Indie moving around the family room in the basement. There was a master suite down here. He had intended for them to sleep together there but wasn't sure yet of her state of mind.

She didn't like being vulnerable.

So he waited.

And that waiting paid off.

He first heard then felt her sit to the side of him on the recliner. She then snuggled against him, resting her head on his shoulder.

Wes gently wrapped his arm around her and then pressed a kiss to the side of her head.

"What if I can't catch him?" she asked.

The confirmation of her uncertainty arrowed

through him. Most of the time she was strong. Her doubt made her human.

"You will." He ran his fingers over her hair, keeping his lips close, breathing in her flowery scent. "You're stronger than that, Indie. He can't hurt you now. We'll find a way to get him."

She tipped her head up and met his eyes. He hoped his sincerity showed.

Long seconds passed. He could see how relaxed she became, gazing into his eyes, warming him... and more.

When she urged him for something deeper, he kissed her a little harder and glided his tongue with hers. Her hand slid up his chest, going between the open part at the top of his shirt and touching his chest. He kept his hand on her hip, letting her set the pace.

They were less than an inch apart from each other. He could feel and smell her sweet breath and the light body spray she used.

Going up onto her knees, Indie straddled him and leaned down to continue the lovemaking of their mouths. He cupped her butt cheeks with each of his hands. Her hair tickled his face and neck.

Suddenly she tore the buttons of his shirt to expose his torso. Wes had to restrain himself from taking over. Everything inside of him struggled not to lift her, plant her onto the sofa next to them and get on top of her.

He endured her hands on him, and then her mouth and tongue, which faithfully followed the caressing trail. When she moved lower, over his abdomen and close to dangerous terrain, he knew he was on the verge of losing all control. Grunting softly, he put his hands on each side of her head and gently made her look at him. She was on fire and he sensed this was not like her. Did she really want this? He had to be sure.

"Is this because you're vulnerable tonight?" he asked.

She breathed a little heavier in reaction but her eyes lost no passion. "Maybe. I honestly don't know. All I do know is I feel something so strong with you. I can't deny that. I may need this because I'm vulnerable, but there is no other man I'd rather be with right now. There's *no one* I'd rather be with right now."

He appreciated her honesty. While he still felt at risk of a broken heart, or at the very least, another dismal disappointment, he accepted her terms.

"Then let's take this to a more appropriate setting," he said, and lifted her into his arms.

Indie thought he was being incredibly romantic by carrying her to his bedroom. She had grown to love this room, not just for its masculine aura, but for the way it spoke to her about the man who slept here. She smelled him everywhere. She smelled his cologne, his antiperspirant. All subtle and pleasant. All man.

Wes let her feet to the floor and they stood before each other. Awkwardness and her usual trepidation that embarking into an intense relationship—or one that could potentially be terribly wrong—tinged her, but only peripherally.

With his heated, sexy, cautiously lustful eyes, he began undressing. He made her so hot she did the same. They undressed together.

Wes waited. Indie didn't catch on as to why, until she realized he was waiting for her again. For her permission. Apparently she called the shots.

This was new to her. She realized if she was ever going to overcome her past, she'd have to take chances.

Most men she was with tried all they could to get into her pants.

Not Wes. How enlightening. He was not the austere, unsociable cowboy the community had—for the most part—pegged him for.

Indie went to the bed and yanked back the covers. She pulled them back far enough for both of them. Then she crawled onto the cool, soft bed, stretching out on her side.

His eyelids lowered, hooding eyes full of manly intent.

Indie never got tired of glancing at his manhood. He was not overly large. He had girth and enough length to satisfy. Inches did matter, but they mattered only in the context of fit.

"Are you sure about this?" he asked, his insecurity coming out again.

Wes was not insecure. Not as a *man*. But he was insecure about women. That Indie understood. She'd been through hell in past relationships. She felt like a moron for making bad decisions. Wes, she knew, was the same. Maybe that was why she was so drawn to him.

"No." She answered honestly. "But I feel too strongly to deny this."

His intensity softened to something warm and trusting. Indie was a little reticent about that until he got onto the bed and lay beside her. Propping his head up, he just looked at her.

Oh.

She continued to meet his gaze. Warmth built. A sweet connection.

Then he lowered his face and she tilted her head so their lips met. Soft. Not moving.

Instant fire ignited in her. She heard and felt his breathing go faster. Then she slid her hand to the back of his neck. The kiss intensified. She opened to his urging pressure.

His hand glided from the side of her breast down over the curve of her hip to her rear. He pulled her closer.

Indie took the hint and moved on top of him. She was intent on indulging herself with him. No past baggage holding her back. Call it a test.

He was so hard. She rubbed herself against him, waiting for her mind to ruin it all.

It didn't.

He engaged her without even trying. Or maybe it was her who didn't have to try.

Anymore.

The fright of that thought was drowned by Wes

easing her thighs open. He positioned himself at her opening and slowly penetrated.

His hands holding her knees on the underside, keeping them up, sent hot flashes of passion through her. It took a lot of trust for a woman to enjoy that… at least for her.

Putting her hands on his muscular chest, she began moving her hips. Immediately she saw the result in Wes. He gripped her hips, encouraging her.

He met her movements, catching her sensitive spot. Amazingly, he knew how to get the angle right. Every time.

She came hard and he followed seconds later.

Indie stayed on top of him while the sensations subsided. She still met his eyes and watched as they became less predatory in a sexual sense. A man loving his woman, but a man who was wired to procreate.

She loved that.

"Come here," Wes murmured, guiding her alongside him.

She curled up next to him, warm and full of love.

The next night, Wes wore a blond wig and Indie wore a short-haired red one; they had glasses and dressed a little raggedy. DAI had provided an old, rusty Subaru. They were a couple of hippies. He had suffered gut-level laughter over their disguises, and so had Indie. Wes couldn't remember ever having so much fun. Now they were on the prowl, about to face danger. Danger wasn't part of his ranch life other than natural predators going after his livestock. That was completely different.

And then…not.

Wes would do whatever it took to keep his livestock safe. He wasn't afraid of predators, be they animal or human. He hadn't made that connection or analogy until now, after meeting Indie. She had opened his mind and world to so much more than he had been exposed to previously. She made him realize things about himself he doubted he would have otherwise.

Aaron had been easy to find. His car was parked outside a twenty-four-hour diner. After thirty minutes, he emerged, looking around, glancing toward them and then moving on apparently without recognition. Their disguises had worked.

Giving him a few seconds' lead, Wes drove to follow.

About fifteen minutes later, Aaron pulled into a gas station and parked. Wes parked across the street. Aaron stayed in his car, watching the gas station. Wes could see movement inside. A woman spoke with a man behind the checkout counter and then slung a purse over her shoulder. It looked like a shift change.

Aaron must have been watching this woman for a while because he had to know her shift was ending right now.

Sure enough, the woman emerged and walked to her car, an older white Honda Civic. She wasn't Juliet.

Was this a new target?

The woman drove away from the station and Aaron followed.

"Give him a few seconds," Indie said.

"Yeah. Got it." Wes waited and then followed a good distance behind. The woman drove about ten minutes to a mediocre apartment building, dark brick with little to brag about, though it appeared clean and secure.

Aaron pulled into the parking lot and parked a few spaces away from the woman. He turned off his headlights and got out.

Indie climbed out of their old Subaru and headed toward Aaron. Alarmed, Wes trailed her, wishing he had something smaller than a rifle. Damn if he'd let her go into a perilous situation without him, though. He kept the rifle close to his side, seeing she had her hand on her holstered pistol.

Aaron disappeared in a stairwell where the woman had gone. Wes stayed in the shadows while Indie pointed her weapon up the stairs. She turned front and backward as she climbed.

Wes followed, searching for any threats. He heard footsteps above and then a door closing, followed by a subtle snap of a dead bolt.

On the second level, he saw Indie follow a dark figure, who took another stairway down to the parking lot. She bent over to look down, gun aimed, but straightened shortly thereafter.

"Aaron's gone," she said, and went to the gas station worker's door and pounded. "He didn't see us.

He must have just wanted to know where this woman lived."

She held her PI badge up for the peep window.

The door opened a crack, revealing a blue-eyed beauty with long, dark hair.

"I'm Indie Deboe, PI. I've been tracking a suspect who just followed you here."

"Wha…?" The woman's mouth fell open and her eyes grew fearful as she looked up and down the passageway. "Who?"

"May we come in?" Indie asked.

She looked at Wes. "Who's he?"

"He's…my partner."

Wes liked that she called him her partner, but he suspected she meant something entirely different than she presented to the woman. After last night, neither of them could deny they were more than friends or casual acquaintances.

Inside the small apartment, they stood near the door.

"Who followed me?" the woman asked. "And why?"

"Could you tell us your name, please?" Indie asked, pulling out a small notepad and pen from her light jacket pocket.

"Phoebe. Phoebe Kaufman."

"How old are you, Phoebe?" Indie asked.

"Twenty-four."

"How long have you worked at the gas station?" Indie jotted the woman's age down.

"Six months. I'm in college."

Indie smiled. "Good for you. Do you have family nearby?"

"Why is all that relevant? Who followed me and why?" Phoebe became more insistent.

Indie drew in a breath and let it out slowly, obviously reluctant to tell this woman she had a dangerous serial killer watching her. "His name is Aaron Bennett. He's stalked, raped and murdered several women. We only just recently discovered his identity and now we're trying to apprehend him so police can make an arrest."

"A *serial killer*?" Phoebe put her hand to her mouth for a few seconds, then looked at Indie. "How long has he been watching me?"

"Probably several weeks. He knows we're onto him."

"Oh my…"

"Do you have family nearby? Friends?" Indie asked.

"I have friends in college. My family lives in California."

"Could you stay with one of your friends for a while? If you give me your cell number, I'll call you as soon as we've caught him."

"Yes. Of course." She went to get a sticky note pad and began writing.

"There will be police detectives who will want to talk to you. They'll ask you if you've noticed anything suspicious or different and will show you a picture of the suspect. That might trigger a memory for you." Indie smiled sympathetically. "I suggest you get packed and leave tonight. I'll arrange for a patrol car to keep an eye on your building for tonight."

"Okay."

Wes could see Indie didn't want to leave the woman alone, but if they had any chance of catching Aaron, they had to move fast.

After a while on the road, Indie's cell rang. Not recognizing the number, but not seeing a spam alert, she answered. "Deboe."

"Ms. Deboe," a dark, raspy voice said, sarcastic and arrogant.

Instantly she knew who it was. She stopped walking. "Aaron. How nice of you to call."

She looked at Wes, who appeared anxious to know what was being said. She pressed the speaker.

"Did you think dressing up in your cute disguises would fool me?" Aaron asked.

"You saw us?"

"I am always on the lookout for you, Indiana Deboe. It's been a delight working against someone of your stature. Your reputation is quite flattering to me."

Indie began to fear he had deliberately led them to Phoebe's apartment to throw them off. "Where are you now?"

"Wouldn't you love to know. But I'll give you a hint." Speaking to someone else in what sounded like his running car, he said, "Say hello to the detective who will never be able to save you."

Aaron must have removed a gag of some sort because now Indie, along with Wes, heard the frightened breaths of a woman followed by her voice. "Please. Help me!" she pleaded.

Indie had a sick feeling he had just abducted Juliet Williams. Had she left her house? She must have. Maybe she felt safe after some time had passed with no sign of him. But Aaron was very good at staying invisible. In fact, he took pride in his abilities.

"Isn't that sweet?" Aaron said.

"We're on Main Street heading into town!" Juliet cried out.

"Shut your mouth!" The sound of a thump told Indie he had just knocked the woman with something, and hard enough to silence her.

"Going somewhere in town?" Indie asked. Where?"

He laughed sinisterly. "You mean you can't figure that out on your own? Not even a hotshot like you can catch me. This is going to be more fun than I expected."

Indie said nothing. She let the arrogant man think he was invincible, that he had outsmarted them. It was going to his head. Where once he was threatened, now he felt empowered. That would be his downfall.

Chapter 16

After Aaron ended the call, Indie stared at her phone, thinking.

"He went to kidnap Juliet while we were talking with Phoebe," Wes said. "Where in town would he take her?"

"He's not taking her to town," she responded, looking up at his handsome face. "He's taking her to that abandoned cabin. It's not a crime scene anymore."

"Why would he take her to a place we know about?"

"He's trying to throw us off again. He thinks we'll be searching all over town while he's up at the same cabin where he took me, raping and killing another woman. He's probably thrilled with the idea, fantasizing how devastated I'll be knowing this time he succeeded."

Wes met her eyes a moment, thinking along with her. "He failed with you, so now he wants to show you he can still get away with his crime."

Indie nodded. Nothing would make the killer happier, more satisfied, impressed with himself.

Wes did not want Indie to go to the abandoned cabin ahead of Radcliff's team. She had called the detective on the way. He knew she was capable but he couldn't stave off his natural male instinct to protect her. The cabin was about a forty-five-minute drive from where they were. He worried that they wouldn't make it in time to save Juliet.

He imagined the woman's terror when Aaron turned his car around and told her no help was coming for her.

Wes turned onto the road leading to the cabin and parked near the driveway, out of sight. Then he and Indie left the car and started for the driveway. As they neared the cabin, they tried to stay out of view, using the trees for cover. There were lights on inside the derelict wooden structure.

Gun ready, Indie slowly approached the first window and carefully peered through it. She recognized the small kitchen area. Moving a little to the right, she could see most of the living room. A ripped-up couch and an old rickety side table with a dim light were the only decorations. No one was in there.

"He must have taken her back to one of the bedrooms." There were two. "Come on, let's go around to the back."

Quietly, they crept along the side of the cabin. Around back, Indie stopped at the back window of the room where Aaron had taken her.

A loud, piercing scream reverberated through the walls and window.

Indie glanced back at Wes and they shared a sickening truth. Aaron had begun his ritualistic torture of the woman.

She hoped they weren't too late.

"Let's go in from the front," Wes said. "I saw a patio on the side when we approached. If the front is locked we can try that."

"Good thinking," Indie said.

They hurried to the front and Wes tested the door. It was open. Indie doubted the lock even worked anymore.

Armed with his rifle and her pistol, they entered. Wes aimed down the hall while Indie cleared the living room and kitchen. A feeling of dread slipped over her as she found herself recalling what had happened the last time she was here. Shaking that off, she focused on the job.

Hearing Juliet crying and pleading, Indie hurried down the hall to the bedroom. In the doorway, she saw Aaron in the process of removing his victim's clothing.

"Step away and put your hands on your head!" she shouted.

A surprised Aaron turned to look at her. Juliet scrambled off the bed and ran toward Indie, bumping her as she passed. The temporary interruption gave him a chance to retaliate. He did so by throwing the knife he held at her. Indie ducked and Wes jumped to the side as the blade struck the hallway wall.

In the next instant, Aaron knocked Indie's gun from her hand and swept his leg under her feet, causing her to fall to the floor. Wes hit Aaron's head with the butt of his rifle, but the maniac moved in time to avoid serious damage. Aaron then kicked Wes's knee, sending him backward and falling into the hallway.

Indie scrambled for her gun but it was too far out of reach. Aaron kicked her hard on her side. She cried out and tried to reach her gun but he got there first. He turned it on her, barrel aiming for her head, but Wes rammed into him, knocking him down.

But not before Indie felt a bullet drive through her torso. She didn't know where, or if any vital organs were compromised, but the force threw her back against the wall. She put her hand over the source of blood gushing from her. Soon she felt light-headed. Weak. Vaguely she could process what was going on between Wes and Aaron. Wes had pried the gun from Aaron's fingers and now pummeled him with his fists.

One last hard punch, and Aaron went unconscious.

Indie knew she was losing a lot of blood. But she still managed to give Wes the handcuffs she always carried.

"Indie." His worried voice told her he cared more about her than defusing Aaron.

"Cuff him," she said, and then everything went black.

After cuffing the psychopath, Wes used his phone to call for emergency help, grateful he had service. They were close enough to the highway, apparently. Either that or his provider had great coverage.

He kicked Aaron twice in the head with his pointy-toed cowboy boots—just to be sure he'd stay unconscious—and as payback for shooting Indie. Taking off his shirt, he found Indie's wound and pressed hard. It was in her abdomen. Not good. A flash of pure fear singed her. She didn't have much time. Securing the makeshift bandage, and checking her pulse and breathing, he felt okay about leaving her for a few seconds.

He ran out of the cabin in search of Juliet. She was nowhere in sight. At least she got away. He worried that in her panicked state she'd get lost, but his first priority was Indie. Seconds mattered. He rushed back to her.

Thankfully, he heard sirens just minutes later. Looking out the window in front, he saw police cars come to a stop close to the cabin and the ambulance keeping its distance, lights flashing.

Aaron began to stir. Wes stood and went to him, giving him a couple of more kicks to the head. Then he went to the door and opened it for the sheriff and his deputies. They entered with guns drawn.

"Indie needs medical attention right away," Wes said.

One of the deputies searched Aaron, who moaned.

The sheriff radioed for paramedics to come in.

They made a lot of noise in their urgency, which Wes appreciated. He stood aside as they went to work on Indie, doing their best to stabilize her before putting her on the gurney. He felt helpless and full of worry.

Wes had to stay behind to talk to the sheriff and his team. All he wanted to do was rush to the hospital. Radcliff arrived a few minutes later.

"Mr. McCann." Radcliff shook his hand. Then he turned his attention to the sheriff. "I have a crime scene team on the way. I'll talk to Wes on the way to the hospital."

The sheriff nodded. "We'll stay here until everything is wrapped up."

Radcliff took a few minutes to peruse the crime scene, jotting down some notes. "Indie will want me to fill her in on the crime scene." He turned to the sheriff. "Could you make sure you send everything you find over to me?"

"Absolutely."

Wes kept checking the time, torn apart with worry. Was Indie all right?

Finally Wes joined Radcliff in his vehicle and they were on their way to the hospital, a portable police light atop the unmarked car.

"Your lady is quite a woman," Radcliff said as he

raced down the highway toward the hospital. "Smart. Professional."

"She was shot," was all Wes could say.

"That's the risk we all take. She caught her man, though."

Wes glanced at the detective. He got that Radcliff respected Indie, but Wes did not like that the woman he could probably spend the rest of his days with had risked her life. He could not take another loss like that.

"I know all about her family," Radcliff went on, still looking ahead at the road. "She has a real purpose doing what she does."

Wes turned to the side window, unable to refute that.

"She'll make it through," Radcliff said. "That girl is a fighter. She fights for justice. For what's right."

She did. Indie was not only tough, smart and professional, she had a pure heart and soul. She was everything he'd ever wanted in a woman, but had not found until now.

"Did they find Juliet?" he asked.

"They're looking for her," Radcliff said, nodding to his radio. "They'll tell me when she's found."

"*If* she's found."

"No. *When* she's found. She can't have gone far."

Indie had found her way to the diner. Maybe Juliet would, too. "She must be terrified beyond belief right now."

"She got away. She's not as terrified as she was when you and your girlfriend saved her," Radcliff said.

Wes looked at him and for once the detective met his gaze, if only briefly. Wes and Indie had saved her. If Indie hadn't anticipated Aaron's next move, Juliet would have died tonight.

"Ms. Deboe is going to be fine," Radcliff reiterated. Then he pulled into the emergency entrance of the local hospital and parked.

They both left the car.

"I'm going to go sit outside Aaron's room," Radcliff said. "I want to be there when they're finished with him."

Aaron had to receive medical care before he was released into the custody of police. "That's good to know."

"He won't get away. I promise," Radcliff said.

"I trust you. Indie trusts you."

Radcliff smiled slightly, almost grimly. "I'll find you."

He nodded and they entered the emergency center, Wes heading for Indie, Radcliff heading for a senseless murderer.

Wes found out shortly after entering the ER that Indie had been taken into surgery. He sat in the waiting room, beside himself with worry. He ran his fingers through his hair countless times. Drank four cups of coffee. Paced. Went outside for fresh air. Anything to calm his mind. If she died, he would want to die himself. She meant everything to him. He realized that now, with terrifying clarity. He had never met a woman more suited for him, a woman who had opened his mind and heart like no other.

As he walked along the sidewalk in front of the hospital, he heard clicking shoes, a woman running in high heels. He turned and saw—to his utter shock—Charlotte rushing toward him.

"Wes?" she said, concern making her voice high-pitched. "Oh, Wes." She reached him and threw her arms around him. "I heard what happened. Are you okay?" She leaned back.

How had she heard? Was it already on the news?

Looking at her he saw plasticity. More likely she'd been keeping tabs on him from afar. She'd kept her distance until now, but she must have an ulterior motive for that.

Why had he never, before meeting Indie, seen Charlotte for what she really was? She wasn't real. She cared about money and material things. He wasn't a vain man, but he had a gut feeling all this woman needed was a good-looking man, maybe a rugged one. A rancher, even though she hated ranch life. It was what others saw that mattered to her. He felt stupid for letting her into his life.

"Why are you here?" he asked flatly.

"I heard that the detective I saw you with at the ranch was shot and that the serial rapist and murderer was caught. My goodness, Wes, were you with her when all that happened?"

"Why are you here?" he repeated.

"I was worried. I needed to make sure you were all right," she said.

More like she needed to try and worm her way back into his life. He spread his arms out. "Well, you can see I am all right." He turned and started back toward the hospital entrance.

So much for some peaceful fresh air.

"Wes." Charlotte took hold of his arm.

He stopped and faced her. "Charlotte…" He sighed.

Letting go of his arm, she folded hers in front of her, searching his face.

Wes calmed. He wasn't a man who'd hurt a woman with harsh words, although he had a few in mind for her. "Come on. Why are you *really* here, Charlotte?"

She blinked a few times. "Are you working with her?"

"Indie? No."

"Are…are you intimate?" she asked.

Wes didn't answer. As far as he was concerned, that was none of her business.

"Wes?"

"She's a good person," was all he had to say.

"Oh…" Charlotte looked down, seeming to gather herself. She must have read between the lines about the true nature of their relationship. Then she looked up and met his eyes. "Is she going to be all right?"

Wes cocked his head. "Just how did you hear about what happened?" And so fast. It couldn't have been just the news.

He immediately saw her hesitation. "Charlotte…?"

"I… I've been talking with Detective Radcliff."

Oh, really. Wes felt even more stupid for letting this woman into his life.

"I had a good reason, Wes," she said. "I was concerned about you falling for Indiana Deboe."

Early on, maybe, but now Radcliff respected Indie. He waited for his ex to continue.

"She was married before," Charlotte said. Blurted, more like.

"Yeah. She told me."

Charlotte looked momentarily confused. "She did?"

"Yes. Charlotte, you have to stop trying to make us get back together. It is never going to happen."

"But…did she tell you she had an affair with a married man?"

That struck all kinds of emotional chords in Wes. Charlotte had cheated on him and he had almost forgiven her. Indie said a cop had helped her get away from Cole. Her ex.

"Russ was married?" he forced himself to ask.

"Yes."

Wes hated her for the self-gratifying grin that formed on her face.

"She didn't tell you?"

"Not that part," he said. "But why does that matter to you? You slept with another man when you were married to me."

Charlotte did her best to feign innocence. "That meant nothing. It was just sex. It's still you I want, Wes."

"And my horse ranch?" he spat.

She put her hand on his chest. "That doesn't matter. All that matters is you. I realize that now. I made a mistake."

"You don't even like horses." Wes walked away.

"She's not the one for you, Wes. I am."

Back in the hospital, Wes waited, mentally and physically spent, for the doctor to come out of surgery. He just wanted to go home and have a couple of whiskeys.

"Mr. McCann?"

Wes looked up to see Indie's doctor approach.

He stood, anxious and full of conflicting emotions. *Indie had an affair with a married man...and she hadn't told him. .*

Her betrayal cut deep but concern for her recovery outweighed that right now. "She made it through the surgery. We had to remove a small portion of her intestines but she should recover just fine. She's going to be sedated for a while. Might be best for you to go home and get some rest. Come back in the morning."

Wes nodded, a powerful wave of relief washing through him. Indie was going to be all right. "Thank you, Doctor."

"Does she have any other family?" the surgeon asked.

Feeling a pang of remorse, he said, "No."

"Oh." The man nodded solemnly. "Well, good thing she has you."

Wes had no family, either. He felt betrayed by the one person who might have changed his life forever. "I'll call her employer in the morning."

Guess it was back to hardening himself and delving into his ranch. He didn't want any woman in his life. And he wasn't sure he ever would again.

As he left, Wes didn't think he had ever felt so empty in his entire life. He had grown to trust Indie, but she had withheld crucial details of her past from him. Her having an affair with a married man pierced through his soul. His ex had done that to him. He had been blinded by the ideology of wife and family and had almost dismissed the significance. But it mattered. It mattered if the woman he was with was trustworthy enough for that lifestyle. And he wanted that more than anything. It had taken him a long time to come to terms with that. Indie had made him see that. And now she was a woman like his ex.

Granted, she had been in a bad relationship and the cop had helped her, but she should have told him everything. The fact that she hadn't destroyed his trust in her.

Indie woke to dim light. She felt groggy and her abdomen hurt terribly. Looking around with blurry eyes, she saw no one in the room. Where was she?

The machine to her left and the IV brought everything crashing back in vivid memory. Aaron had shot her. What had happened to Wes? Was he in another hospital room? Where was Juliet?

"Wes?" she called out, her voice coarse and weak. She dropped her head back onto the pillow, completely exhausted.

"Ah. You're awake."

Indie saw a male nurse approach her bed.

"Wes. Juliet." She could barely get the words out.

"You came out of anesthesia pretty slow," the nurse said. "How are you feeling?"

"Pain," she said. "Where is Wes?"

"Who?"

"Wes McCann."

"Only one person has been here since you were brought up to your room," he said. "He brought flowers."

Indie saw the flowers next to her on the windowsill. The nurse brought her the card. They were from Julien and everyone else at DAI.

Wes hadn't come to her room? "Is he okay?" Had he been shot? Where was he?

"Juliet?"

"There was a Detective Radcliff that asked about you. But no one else has been in here. Do you want me to call someone?"

"I need to know if Wes is okay. And Juliet."

"Okay, let me do some checking. That detective gave me a card."

"Call him now."

The nurse did as she asked and soon he spoke with Detective Radcliff. "He says he'd like to talk to you."

Indie took the phone with her right hand, the one that didn't have the IV in it. "Detective?"

"Indie?" Radcliff said in a beaming voice. "I'm so glad to hear your voice!"

"Is Wes okay?" she asked. "Juliet?"

"Yes. I brought Wes to the hospital." He paused.

"Is he not there?" What was wrong? She would have thought he would be here.

"No. He left before I came to recovery."

"The doctor said he told him to go home and get some rest. He's fine, though. And Aaron is in jail now. He was released from the hospital early this morning."

"Juliet?"

"I found her. She is fine, too. Resting at home," he said.

Indie let her head relax against the pillow, realizing she had tensed up. She closed her eyes. "That's all good to hear." Except for Wes. Why wasn't he here?

"All thanks to you."

The nurse had injected something into her IV and she began to feel drowsy.

"It wasn't all me," she said.

"You are entirely too humble, my dear. You get some rest. Everything is going to be okay."

"Where is Juliet?"

"Home. Resting, like I said. I talked to her. She's alive because of you."

His respectful, soft voice relaxed her. Everyone was okay.

"Thank you, Detective," she mumbled.

"Go to sleep, Indie. I'll come by in the morning."

Indie fell into a soft slumber, induced by drugs that dulled her concern about Wes.

Chapter 17

Indie was surprised to see Jacey Cruz standing outside the hospital. Indie had been released, drugged up on pain meds and in hand with follow-up instructions that included physical therapy.

Where was Wes? Why hadn't he come to get her?

Jacey and the nurse helped her into the Jeep Grand Cherokee, the activity nearly making Indie vomit from pain and exhaustion.

She rested her head against the seat, breathing like a ninety-year-old.

"Kadin sent me," Jacey said.

"Where is Wes?"

"I don't know. Kadin just asked me to get you and bring you home."

Why her?

She must have drifted off, because she was only vaguely aware of someone carrying her into a bedroom, where she promptly fell into a deep, dreamless sleep.

Indie didn't know how long she had been out, but when she opened her eyes she saw Jacey sitting on the chair next to her bed. Where was Wes? Her gunshot wound hurt terribly.

"Welcome back, sleepyhead," Jacey said. "You've been out for several hours. You must be in pain." She retrieved a prescription container from the nightstand and handed Indie a bottle of water.

Indie took the meds. "Why are you doing this?"

"Kadin asked me to," she said.

That was too simple. Indie didn't know this woman at all. She had only met her once. Was she running from something and did Kadin know? Indie was no stranger to complicated pasts.

"Are you hiding from someone?" Indie asked.

Jacey's face lit up with a brilliant smile. "Kadin said you had some sort of a sixth sense. That you are a smart, intuitive detective."

"And?"

"All I can tell you is this works for me right now. I'm helping you and you're helping me."

"And Kadin knows why?"

"You get some rest, Indie. Now that I know you woke and have your meds, I can get some rest of my own."

"Wait. Has Wes called?" She glanced around for her cell and saw it on the side table.

"Not that I'm aware. Kadin didn't tell me about your relationship with someone named Wes."

He'd just told her to get her from the hospital and stay with her, somewhere no one would know.

"Thanks for the help," Indie said with no shortage of sarcasm. What was going on with Wes? He seemed to have abandoned her. Why? What had happened? She was plagued with not knowing. Should she call him?

At the bedroom door, Jacey looked back. "We'll talk more later. I have a case I'd like to discuss."

"Oh. Sure." Indie didn't relent on her sarcasm. Kadin had more motive than giving this woman a safety net. He wanted her to get Indie's take on a case.

She could live with that. Her curiosity grew, though, over why Jacey appeared to be on the run.

What she couldn't live with was Wes's mysterious vanishing. When Jacey left the room, she picked up her cell and called him, a little peeved that he hadn't so much as checked up on her.

He didn't answer, so she kept calling until he finally did.

"Wes?"

"Indie. I made sure you were going to be all right before I left the hospital," he said. It sounded like the excuse it was. She had never heard so much coldness in his tone. He'd had a similar coarseness when she first met him at Julien's engagement party, but this sounded much more emotionally charged.

"What happened?' Indie asked.

"You got shot. Aaron is no longer a threat. You don't need me anymore," he said.

What the…

She decided not to remind him that she never did need him. Not with her case.

"Wes. What *happened?"* she asked.

"You *lied.* That's what happened," he bit out.

Indie tried to figure out why he thought she had lied. "About what?"

"Russ. Charlotte told me all about him."

Charlotte. That vindictive, jealous woman. Had she twisted her relationship with Russ? She must have made a special effort to dig into Indie's past and present it in a new light to Wes. She wanted Wes back, but for selfish reasons.

"You don't know the whole story. Charlotte will say anything to reunite with you."

"Are you saying what she told me isn't true?" Wes asked.

"No. Russ did help me escape, and I did have an affair with him." This was the part she never liked rehashing. "My ex-husband, Cole, was charming and sweet when I first met him, but after we married I began to realize he had a temper, and not the normal bouts of temper people have every once in a while. He got physical when I verbally fought back. I told you the truth about that. He had to have control over me, where I went and when and with whom. He didn't like me going anywhere without him. It was like he had to always track me and dictate what I said and did."

She shook her head, feeling sick to her stomach. "The next time he hit me I called the police. Remember I mentioned to you one of the officers who responded was Russ? Well, anyway, he told me about his sister, how she had gotten into a relationship like that. He warned me that if I didn't get away right then, Cole would continue to haunt me. I believed him. He helped me escape, put me up in his carriage house. Cole found me and Russ intervened." She paused. "Did Charlotte tell you about the restraining order?"

"No. But you never told me he was married," Wes said. "You deliberately hid that from me."

Indie sighed. This would not make her appear honorable. "Yes. True. I didn't tell you that. I'm not proud of it, but in my defense, I wasn't in a good place back then. I know I was wrong for not telling you, but it has always been very hard for me to talk about. It was another huge loss for me. I lost my family, Wes. Everything I told you except for my affair with Russ was all true. I'm sorry. I just couldn't talk about it. I wasn't good at that. I'm still not." She released a quavering breath. "I know that doesn't absolve me, but that's just the way it is. You are the only person I have ever told about Cole and Russ. Kadin didn't even ask. He just knew I needed a break. For once in my life. He also knew I was worth it."

Indie had a valid reason for straying. She was in a bad marriage. But still. She had an affair with a married man. Charlotte had an affair while she was still married to Wes. Indie knew he had taken time to come to the realization that his wife wasn't worth keeping. He wanted a family. Now Indie had crushed his trust in her.

"You didn't have to leap into another relationship," he said, his voice softening. Was that a good sign? "You could have just gotten away from your husband."

"I did get away from him and that would not have happened without Russ. Like I said, I was vulnerable. My affair with Russ didn't last. I ended it and moved here."

"Why didn't you tell me everything?" Wes asked, more like demanded.

Indie had to take a few calming breaths. This could mean the end of them. She found she did not want that. Not at all.

"Because I knew Charlotte cheated on you and you had a similar past to my own when it comes to family. And… I didn't really know you that well. Everything happened so fast between us. I… I was scared and I guess I wanted to see if what we had was worth pursuing."

"Is it?" he asked.

"Yes." She meant that with all her heart.

"When did you realize that?"

Not until now. That sent her heart plummeting. He wouldn't believe her. "Right now, Wes. There was too much going on with my case before. And I don't trust easily." She squeezed her eyes shut, waiting.

Several seconds later, he said, "I need some time to think about all this."

"Okay. Take all the time you need," she said, each

word breaking her. She was so accustomed to being on her own, not risking depending on others, that she had to preserve what she could of her emotional state. She didn't want him to withdraw, but she had to let him go. For now.

Indie broke down in tears.

Moments later, when she had time to gather herself, Jacey opened the door with a tray of food and wine. She put the tray on the bed and Indie saw it was full of grapes, cheese and crackers.

"Can't have wine on an empty stomach," Jacey said.

Indie realized this was one unconventional woman. She'd just given her pain meds and now wine and cheese.

Jacey handed her a tissue. "Don't waste your energy on men who don't see you for who you really are."

Indie took the partially filled glass of wine. "Who *are* you?"

Jacey smiled and held up her own glass of wine. "I'm a friend." She sipped and then added, "I'm also someone who shares a similar background to you."

"Kadin told you?"

"He never invaded your privacy, but, yes, he told me enough. I didn't tell him much about me, either. But he knew." She took another sip.

That bastard. But a good-hearted bastard. Indie could never fault him.

"Who are you trying to get away from?" she asked.

"I can't tell you. No one can know where I am or

who I befriend or work with. Not yet. Please don't question me on that. Just know I am a detective and only Kadin is privy to my work background. He knows very little about my personal background, though, and that is the way it needs to stay."

Indie studied this new, unexpected friend. "You and I do have something in common. But I think you are in much more danger than I ever was."

"You lost your entire family. I'm trying not to lose mine."

Indie had a new respect for this woman. Jacey was so beautiful and strong. She wanted to get to know her better.

"Is there a case you want to discuss?" Indie asked.

"Yes, but not now. You get well. We aren't going to lose touch anytime soon."

That pricked Indie's interest no small amount, but the few sips of wine she had made her drowsy, something she guessed Jacey had planned. She must have heard her call with Wes. The wine would send her into sleep. Painless sleep.

Wes had had maybe two hours of sleep last night. He gulped his first sip from a second cup of dark black coffee. His eyes felt puffy and he was fatigued.

Charlotte had left him alone after he'd told her even if Indie turned out to be a no-go he would never be with her ever again. But what Charlotte had told him was true. Indie had cheated. Being vulnerable wasn't an excuse. She'd cheated. Wes needed a woman he could trust.

Indie loved the ranch.

That was a bitter pill. A big one.

Charlotte would never be back. She knew Wes would not take her back. She also knew he had more feelings for Indie than he'd ever had for her. The word *love* had never come up, but his ex-wife seemed to have come to the conclusion that Wes was in love with Indie. Really in love. The kind of love he and Charlotte had never had. Wes had difficulty processing that.

The doorbell rang.

Was it Indie?

Wes felt a fool for the thought being forefront. It could not be Indie. She was wounded, in bed and being taken care of by another Dark Alley Investigations detective. Indie's boss had called to tell him, along with some love advice Wes was not ready to hear.

Give her time. She loves you and you love her. You just can't accept it right now.

What was the deal with this agency? They were like a close-knit family and Kadin seemed drawn to those types.

Or was he drawn to types who lost too much?

He stopped those thoughts and headed for the door. Looking through his peephole, he saw a pretty woman who wore a gun and a badge that wasn't official law enforcement.

He opened the door.

"Hi," an exuberant voice said. Too exuberant as far as Wes was concerned.

"I'm Jacey Cruz. I've been taking care of Indie," she said. "May I come in?"

Wes opened the door wider. "Is she all right?"

Jacey stepped inside and turned. "Do you care?"

He couldn't believe she'd asked that. "Yes. Of course I care."

"That's why you're with her at her place?" The woman walked into his home as if she owned it, going to his table, where he had apples in a bowl. She took one and turned to face him, taking a bite.

She was audacious and resembled a rebellious Indie, or a standoffish, defensive one. Or…maybe he was the one who resembled Indie too much. Their backgrounds and personalities. Standoffish. Rebellious. Sometimes defensive. He could not deny he'd been all those things before meeting her.

Wes relaxed, understanding the reason for this visit. "She told you."

"She didn't tell me a damn thing." Jacey took another bite of the apple.

"Kadin did?"

Chewing and then swallowing, taking her sweet time, Jacey said, "He told me all I needed to know. See… Kadin recognizes people who have been wronged in life. He was wronged himself. He will go to any length to get justice, and he hires people who have the same goal…to ferret out the bad people who do harm to the innocent. That's why he doesn't hire just anyone. He hires dedicated detectives."

Detectives with drive and a purpose, with a soul-deep reason for what they do. Wes lowered his head, realizing what a fool he'd been. Wes had losses. Indie had losses. Injustices. She had been thrust into an adult world at a young age. No family. She had to find her own way. Alone. Wes related to that, as they had talked about, but not in enough depth.

He lifted his gaze and met Jacey's head-on. "Why did you come here?"

"You know why."

She was as brash and brazen as she had been since she came through his door. Only she was far from reaching the emotional progress Indie had made. Her defenses, her take-the-bull-by-the-horn attitude said she had toughness, but there was a thick wall around her heart. Indie had been like that.

And so had he.

They had both struggled with the cruelties of life and somehow they had connected. Maybe it was the similarities. It didn't matter. The initial connection had grown into something deeper. Something that frightened both of them.

He realized just then that her affair had been innocent. She was nothing like Charlotte. No comparison. Charlotte wanted the flash of having a real man, but her true passion was material things.

Indie couldn't be farther from that. She was genuine. She cared about people and justice for victims. And she loved his ranch... .

Chapter 18

Wes marched up to Indie's door and checked the handle. It was unlocked. He stormed in, saw Jacey's shocked face from the sofa and went straight for Indie's bedroom. He found her with a bowl of ice cream and a movie playing on her TV. She put the bowl aside with wide, surprised eyes

Throwing the covers off her, he lifted her, careful with her gunshot wound. Then he carried her back through the home.

Passing Jacey, he glanced at her.

A catlike smile pushed up her mouth. "Good man."

Wes scoffed, not liking she had played a big role in his coming here.

"Wes?"

He looked down at Indie's face as he took her to his truck.

"What are you doing?" she asked again.

"Taking you home. Where you belong."

"Home?"

He deposited her into the passenger seat of the truck and remained leaning down, near her. "Yes. Home."

She stared at him, startled and maybe afraid.

"I love you, Indie. I think I fell in love with you the minute I met you."

"Really?" She smiled.

Looking at her beautiful face, all he could do was press a meaningful kiss to her mouth. Then he drew back a bit. "Yes, Indie. I love you."

Tears welled up in her eyes. "Good, because I love you, too. I was afraid you didn't feel the same."

He put his hand to the side of her face. "I know. But I do."

"Oh, Wes." Tears fell down her cheeks. "You have just made me the happiest woman on earth. But... what made you change your mind?"

An honest question. He had to answer. "You're colleague is an interesting woman."

Indie smiled. "She's got some things to work out."

He ran his gaze all over her face. "Like you did?"

"Did?"

"Yes. Did."

She had to take some time to absorb that. "Meaning... I've worked my issues out?"

"When it comes to your past, yes. For the most

part. You will always have that baggage, but you've crossed a threshold Jacey is nowhere near."

"What threshold?" Indie had an idea but she shied away from facing it.

Wes angled his head, cowboy hat shading his face. "Do I really have to say it?"

"You are the first man I've ever met that I truly feel like I can trust with my future."

"I know," he said, drawing her close against him. "Because it's the same for me. I never thought I would meet a woman I could love again."

She tipped her head, thrilled with passion. "I am so looking forward to our future."

"Kids." He grinned.

"Yes. A family."

A real one. Wes was so happy he was near to bursting.

"When do you want to get married?"

"You're not worried it's too soon?" she asked.

"No. Are you?"

She smiled. "No. Then I want to get married as soon as it won't hurt to wear a wedding dress."

Wes put his hand on the side of her face and kissed her.

* * * * *

COMING NEXT MONTH FROM

ROMANTIC SUSPENSE

#2187 COLTON COUNTDOWN
The Coltons of Colorado • by Tara Taylor Quinn
Ezra Colton was only planning to catch up with his family while on leave. But when the twins of the woman he finds himself unable to stop thinking about are kidnapped, he's pulled into a world of conspiracies and fanaticism—while racing against time to save the people who've become like family to him.

#2188 THE SPY SWITCH
by Karen Whiddon
Schoolteacher Jennifer Glass is roped into a dangerous position as an undercover DEA agent when she's mistaken for the twin sister she never knew she had. Actual agent Micah Spokane knows he needs Jennifer's help, but he's determined to keep her safe. Will their electric and unexpected attraction prove to be too distracting?

#2189 KIDNAPPING IN CAMERON GLEN
Cameron Glen • by Beth Cornelison
Jake and Emma Turner's marriage is falling apart. But they set aside all their differences when their teenage daughter Fenn is kidnapped and they have to go deep into dangerous territory to save her—and maybe find a way back to each other.

#2190 THE AGENT'S DEADLY LIAISON
Wyoming Nights • by Jennifer D. Bokal
One night of passion with Marcus Jones led to a pregnancy Chloe Ryder didn't expect. And when a serial killer they captured launches a plan for revenge, Chloe wonders if she'll survive long enough to tell Marcus about their child...

HRSCNM0522

"You think this is a joke? I wonder how many pieces of
you I can cut away before you stop laughing."

On the counter lay a scalpel. Darcy picked it up. The
handle was still stained with Gretchen's lifeblood. Chloe
went cold as she realized that she'd pushed too hard for
information.

Knife in hand, Darcy slowly, slowly approached the
bed. Chloe pressed her back into the pillow, trying in
vain to get distance from the killer and the knife. It did
no good. Darcy pressed Chloe's shackled hand onto the
railing and drew the blade across her palm. The metal
was cold against her skin. She tried to jerk her hand away,
but it was no use.

Darcy drove the blade into Chloe's flesh.

HRSEXP0522

The cut burned, and for a moment, her vision filled with red. Then a seam opened in her hand. Blood began to weep from the wound. She balled her hand into a fist as her palm throbbed, and anger flooded her veins.

Chloe might've been handcuffed to a bed, but that didn't mean that she couldn't fight back.

"Damn you straight to hell," she growled.

With her free hand, Chloe pushed Darcy's chin back. At the same moment, she lifted her feet, kicking the killer in the chest. Darcy stumbled back before tumbling to the ground. Had Chloe been free, she would have had the advantage.

But shackled to the bed? Chloe had done nothing more than enrage a dangerous person.

Standing, Darcy brushed a loose strand of hair from her face. She smiled, then scoffed before echoing Chloe's words. "Damn me to hell? Hell doesn't frighten me, Chloe. Nothing does—especially not you."

Don't miss
The Agent's Deadly Liaison *by Jennifer D. Bokal,*
available July 2022 wherever
Harlequin Romantic Suspense books and
ebooks are sold.

Harlequin.com

HRSEXP0522

Love Harlequin romance?

DISCOVER.

Be the first to find out about promotions,
news and exclusive content!

f Facebook.com/HarlequinBooks

𝕏 Twitter.com/HarlequinBooks

◉ Instagram.com/HarlequinBooks

⊕ Pinterest.com/HarlequinBooks

You Tube YouTube.com/HarlequinBooks

ReaderService.com

EXPLORE.

Sign up for the Harlequin e-newsletter and
download a free book from any series at
TryHarlequin.com

CONNECT.

Join our Harlequin community to
share your thoughts and connect
with other romance readers!
Facebook.com/groups/HarlequinConnection

◈ HARLEQUIN

HSOCIAL2021